Just then a
woman who had
been subject to bleeding for
twelve years came up behind him
and touched the edge of his cloak.
She said to herself, "If I only touch his
cloak, I will be healed."
Jesus turned and saw her. "Take heart,
daughter," he said, "your faith has
healed you." And the woman was
healed at that moment.

—MATTHEW 9:20–22 (NIV)

And a woman was there who had been subject to bleeding for twelve years. She had suffered a great deal under the care of many doctors and had spent all she had, yet instead of getting better she grew worse. When she heard about Jesus, she came up behind him in the crowd and touched his cloak, because she thought, "If I just touch his clothes, I will be healed." Immediately her bleeding stopped and she felt in her body that she was freed from her suffering. At once Jesus realized that power had gone out from him. He turned around in the crowd and asked, "Who touched my clothes?" "You see the people crowding against you," his disciples answered, "and yet you can ask, 'Who touched me?'" But Jesus kept looking around to see who had done it. Then the woman, knowing what had happened to her, came and fell at his feet and, trembling with fear, told him the whole truth. He said to her, "Daughter, your faith has healed you. Go in peace and be freed from your suffering."

—M ARK 5:25–34 (NIV)

As Jesus was on his
way, the crowds almost
crushed him. And a woman was
there who had been subject to bleeding
for twelve years, but no one could heal her. She
came up behind him and touched the edge of his
cloak, and immediately her bleeding stopped. "Who
touched me?" Jesus asked. When they all denied it,
Peter said, "Master, the people are crowding and
pressing against you." But Jesus said, "Someone
touched me; I know that power has gone out from me."
Then the woman, seeing that she could not go
unnoticed, came trembling and fell at his feet. In the
presence of all the people, she told why she had
touched him and how she had been instantly healed.
Then he said to her, "Daughter, your faith has healed
you. Go in peace."

—LUKE 8:42b–48 (NIV)

Ordinary Women of the BIBLE

A MOTHER'S SACRIFICE: JOCHEBED'S STORY
THE HEALER'S TOUCH: TIKVA'S STORY

Ordinary Women of the BIBLE

THE HEALER'S TOUCH

TIKVA'S STORY

❖

CONNILYN COSSETTE

Guideposts

Ordinary Women of the Bible is a trademark of Guideposts.

Published by Guideposts Books & Inspirational Media
100 Reserve Road, Suite E200
Danbury, CT 06810
Guideposts.org

Copyright © 2019 by Guideposts. All rights reserved.

This book, or parts thereof, may not be reproduced, stored in a retrieval system, or transmitted in any form or by any means, electronic, mechanical, photocopying, recording, or otherwise, without the written permission of the publisher.

This is a work of fiction. While the characters and settings are drawn from scripture references and historical accounts, apart from the actual people, events, and locales that figure into the fiction narrative, all other names, characters, places, and events are the creation of the author's imagination or are used fictitiously.

Every attempt has been made to credit the sources of copyrighted material used in this book. If any such acknowledgment has been inadvertently omitted or miscredited, receipt of such information would be appreciated.

Scripture references are from the following sources: *New American Standard Bible (NASB)*. Copyright © 1960, 1962, 1963, 1968, 1971, 1972, 1973, 1975, 1977, 1995 by the Lockman Foundation. Used by permission. *The Holy Bible, New International Version (NIV)*. Copyright © 1973, 1978, 1984, 2011 by Biblica, Inc. Used by permission of Zondervan. All rights reserved worldwide. www.zondervan.com. *Holy Bible, New Living Translation*. Copyright © 1996. Used by permission of Tyndale House Publishers, Inc., Wheaton, Illinois 60189. All rights reserved. Scripture quotations marked *(CEV)* are from the Contemporary English Version Copyright © 1991, 1992, 1995 by American Bible Society. Used by permission.

Cover and interior design by Müllerhaus

Cover illustration by Brian Call and nonfiction illustrations by Nathalie Beauvois, both represented by Illustration Online LLC.

Typeset by Aptara, Inc.

ISBN 978-1-961125-53-7 (hardcover)
ISBN 978-1-961125-54-4 (softcover)
ISBN 978-1-950537-73-0 (epub)

Printed and bound in the United States of America

Ordinary Women of the BIBLE

❖

THE HEALER'S TOUCH

TIKVA'S STORY

For Denise Thayne,
whose unabating grace in deep valleys is an inspiration
and whose generous spirit is an encouragement
to all who are blessed to call her friend.
May Yehovah-Rapha continue to be your source
of hope and strength.

Cast of CHARACTERS

Adina • daughter of Simcha
Agathe • wife of Damianos, the Greek healer
Asa • Tikva's late husband
Chavah • woman traveling with a group to Capernaum to see Jesus and seek healing for her daughter, Na'ami
Damianos • Greek healer
Dara • one of Tikva's maids
Helena • Tikva's mother-in-law
Hiram • part of Chavah's group, traveling to Capernaum to see Jesus
Jairus • a ruler of the synagogue at Capernaum; Jesus restored his daughter to life
Levon • part of Chava's group, traveling to Capernaum to see Jesus; blind in one eye
Lilah • one of Tikva's cousins and closest friends
Margalit • one of Tikva's cousins and closest friends
Medad • trader who sold cheap, imported goods
Meira • one of Helena's friends from the marketplace; traveling to Capernaum with Tikva
Mina • one of Tikva's maids
Na'ami • Chavah's daughter, traveling to Capernaum to find Jesus and seek healing
Nachman • Tikva's father-in-law
Rabbi Shmuel • Tikva's father
Rabbi Yeshua • Jesus

Rachel • Simcha's late wife
Simcha • potter; employs Tikva and Helena; suffers from a twisted foot
Tikva • woman with the issue of blood
Shimon • Simon Peter
Zuri • husband of Meira

Glossary of TERMS

Abba • father
Adonai • Lord
Chazir • pig
Imma • mother
Mikveh • a bath used to perform ritual purification
Niddah • a woman undergoing or who has yet to purify herself following her monthly cycle
Pesach • Passover
Shabbat • Sabbath
Shalom • peace
Shavuot • Feast of Weeks, or Pentecost
Shema • the first two words of Deuteronomy 6 and the title (better known as the Shema) of a prayer that serves as a centerpiece of the morning and evening Jewish prayer services
Shekels • a silver coin and unit of weight used in ancient Israel and the Middle East; money
Tameh • ceremonially unclean
Tanakh • Hebrew Bible
Tzitzit • the strings or fringes of a prayer shawl
Zavah • a state of ritual impurity arising from bleeding that is not during a woman's monthly cycle

PART I

CHAPTER ONE

❖

A mischievous gust of wind whipped Tikva's white headscarf from its mooring. The linen flapped and danced around her like the wings of a tethered dove. With a laugh, she snatched the fabric from the air before it flew out to sea. If only it could drift over the restless waters, search out the one vessel Tikva longed to see, and guide it home. It seemed like years since her Asa had been at sea. Five months was far too long without her husband.

The crash of waves at the foot of the bluff where she stood misted salty droplets over her skin. Breathing in the cool freshness of the ocean breeze, she replaced her headscarf, tucking it securely about her neck and drawing it over her forehead, a buffer against the sparkling glare. Squinting, she continued to peer at the horizon, willing a dark shape to break the line between sky and sea.

She wondered whether she'd ever get used to the tides of life with a man who made his living on the Great Sea. Helena, her husband's mother, had warned her not to stop at the bluff on the way home from the market, saying that the wait would only be prolonged by obsessively watching the horizon for signs of his return—but still, Tikva came, tipping up on her toes and shading her eyes to scan the distance, praying that

Adonai would guide Asa's ship home to Ptolemais with all speed. As the wife of a man who traded far across the expanse, to lands she could barely imagine, she knew she must learn to wait patiently. But surely one could forgive a young bride her anxiety during this first separation. Helena might shake her head and cluck at her daughter-in-law's wringing hands, but Tikva guessed that many years ago it had been Helena standing on this same bluff every afternoon, waiting for Asa's father to slide into port.

Placing a hand on the burgeoning curve of her belly, Tikva repeated her husband's name, hoping that the wind would bear her prayers aloft, straight to the ears of the Almighty. A flutter beneath her palm was the only answer, a silent agreement from the life within that Asa must return as soon as possible. How Tikva longed to see the look on his face when he beheld the mound beneath her tunic, since neither of them had known she was with child five months before when he boarded his ship!

She stroked her fingers across the swell of her middle, dreaming of the day it would be the sweet head of an infant her fingers would caress instead. Would the babe have Asa's deep blue eyes inherited from his Greek mother? His long nose and his sailor's build? Or would he mimic Tikva with her black curls and brown eyes? Asa had talked of little more than a son since their marriage only eight months before, and she longed to place an heir into his arms.

Another swirl of wind tugged at Tikva's skirt, dodging around her ankles like a playful pup, whipping her hair across her eyes. The ocean dipped and swayed, foaming white as it heaved itself against the rocks. She tried not to imagine what the waves might look like far past the breakwater, out beyond the dark clouds that painted the northern sky, nor to remember the tales her father-in-law loved to tell about the fearsome creatures that haunted the deep.

A sprinkle of rain dashed across her cheek, cutting short her vigil. She slipped her market basket higher on her forearm and tucked it close to her body, unwilling to allow the honey cakes she'd purchased from an Egyptian vendor to come to ruin in the sudden rain shower, then plodded down the hill toward the two patient maidservants who waited near the bottom.

Her mother-in-law would shake her head and purse her lips when she returned soaked to the skin, but one of these afternoons Tikva would glimpse a tiny dot on the horizon, one that would grow and grow until her Asa was back in her embrace, and a few gusts of wind and a little rain would mean nothing at all.

CHAPTER TWO

❖

"And where have you been?" Helena demanded the moment Tikva entered the house, as if they did not have this conversation at least twice a week. Although deep into preparations for the Shabbat meal, her light brown hair in a frazzled halo about her face, her mother-in-law was never too busy supervising to chide.

"The market and then the bluff," said Tikva, handing her the basket of the Egyptian honey cakes that she knew Helena was so fond of.

Helena shook her head, mouth pursed as she examined the contents of the basket with not a word of thanks. "It's time to end these excursions, Tikva. You have your babe to consider now. Watching the horizon will not make him return any sooner."

Tikva slid a protective hand over her belly. "I did not exert myself overmuch, I assure you. I would not risk Asa's child for anything."

Helena's glare softened at the name of her precious son. "Be that as it may, you have no need to go to the market, especially on Preparation Day. Too many people milling about. Let Mina and Dara tend to the shopping alone next time."

"I enjoy going with them," Tikva said. "I love to see what new goods have come into port and meeting people from all over the world. Today there was a merchant with linen straight from Egypt, along with the most beautiful turquoise I've ever seen. And the—"

Helena patted her hand, cutting off the description of the wonders Tikva had discovered in the market. "I know you are restless, young as you are. But once the little one comes, you'll have more than enough to fill your time. Now, why don't you go rest for a while until your father and mother arrive? You must not overtire yourself." She handed the basket of rolls to Mina, gesturing for the Phoenician girl to take the treats outside to the kitchen courtyard before swirling off to direct the placement of the flowers that had been gathered from her extensive and well-tended gardens. Helena ran her household with great skill, her servants so attuned to her every wish that she needn't even speak aloud her wishes for them to be fulfilled.

And someday I'll be the mistress of this grand household. The idea thrilled Tikva as much as it made her uneasy. As the daughter of one of the leaders of the synagogue, she'd been by no means poverty stricken, but her father-in-law was one of the wealthiest merchants in Ptolemais. This house was twice the size of the one she'd been born into, with at least ten servants tending to her every need. Tikva had lived here now for the past eight months, since she and Asa had married, but sometimes she still felt like an interloper, one who contributed little to the household at that.

Helena was right that she'd be glad for the babe to be born, not only because she'd be providing Asa with the child he so desperately wanted but because she'd have more to do than wander through the house, wishing he were there. Perhaps when Shabbat was over she would visit Lilah and Margalit, her cousins and closest friends. She'd not seen them for weeks and was desperate for someone her own age with whom she could speak freely.

Unlike Helena, Tikva's mother had insisted she always keep her hands busy when she'd lived at home: cooking, sewing, and cleaning. Her *imma* regarded idleness with nearly as much disdain as she did the beggars that huddled near the gates of the city. Tikva hoped that when her family came for the meal tonight, her mother would not ask what she'd been doing to make herself useful to Helena, because she had no answer.

At least the beggars outside the gates filled their days with the occupation of raising their filthy hands to passersby and lifting their voices to demand alms. Here she was in the way of the bustling servants more often than not, and since Tikva had realized she was with child just after Asa's ship departed, Helena complained anytime she spent more than a few minutes on her feet. As if a short walk through the city and then up a small incline would strip her body of strength.

Annoyed with Helena's overprotectiveness and thankful that, although the day continued to be gray, the rain shower had passed, Tikva slipped out the back door and up the slick stairs to the rooftop, trading hours of lying on her plush bed in boredom for the fresh breeze and the narrow strip of sea view she could snatch between neighboring buildings. It was not the bluff, where the entire blue expanse spread out before her, but it was better than nothing. She pulled a tall stool over to the parapet and sat with her elbows on the wet stone wall.

Then, chin in hand, she took up her vigil, glad that at least this evening her loneliness would be buffered by the presence of her mother and father at the Shabbat meal.

◆

Oil lamps flickered along the length of the table, highlighting the array of lovely dishes Helena's cooks had prepared. Herb-encrusted roasted dove and spicy goat stew lent the room a delicious odor while a vast array of fruits, cheeses, varicolored olives, and freshly baked bread caused Tikva's belly to rumble with anticipation.

Of course, before they could partake in this lovely feast, a blessing must be offered. So with hands outstretched, Tikva's father stood at the head of the table, his deep voice resonant as he recited the familiar words of gratitude to the Ruler of the Universe who created all and sustained all. When, at last, his copious blessings over the food and drink were complete, and he finally folded himself down to recline at the table, Mina and Dara padded into the room to fill everyone's cups with wine.

"Rabbi Shmuel, I am so glad you and Naomi accepted our invitation to join us for the Shabbat meal this evening," said Helena. "I'd hoped that Nachman and Asa would be here to partake with us, but hopefully it will not be much longer before their ship arrives in port."

Tikva's father nodded as he lifted a bite to his lips, barely acknowledging Helena as she spoke. Tikva remembered a time when her father had been effusive with his compliments and smiled widely at men and women alike, but as his status had risen within the synagogue he'd become more and more careful to limit his interactions with those not of his own sex. As a Pharisee, one with a fair amount of influence within Ptolemais and its surrounding areas, he'd become diligent in his observance of the Law, both written and oral, and had taken to heart the admonishments of the learned rabbis against familiarity with women not of his family.

At least he was not like some of his counterparts, who insisted on crossing the street when women came into view, in the off-chance that one of them might be ritually unclean during their monthly time, but still, his slight against Helena, who'd worked so hard to organize such a plentiful table in his honor, grated against Tikva's nerves.

Thankfully, he did not include Tikva in such convictions, even though she was a married woman and no longer a part of his household. As Helena and Tikva's mother discussed the lovely new kidskin sandals her mother had purchased, Tikva's father leaned closer to her, a small smile on his lips.

"Your mother informs me you are with child, Daughter."

"I am," she replied.

"I am pleased to hear it," he said, and her heart trembled with pleasure at his obvious pride. "Perhaps you will fulfill your duty and provide Asa with an heir even before Shavuot next year."

"Yes, Abba. That would be wonderful. Although a daughter would be most pleasant as well." She knew a son was expected of her, and prayed for by her husband, but she did long for a little girl to cherish.

"And just think, your son will inherit all of this," said her father, with a sweep of his palm around the richly appointed room. "Nachman has built quite a reputation in his dealings with Cyprus and Rome. I can imagine that his business will thrive in the years to come. Asa too is a shrewd merchant, like his father. He will pass on quite a legacy to your little one. I knew I made the right choice of husband for you."

She blinked at him, confused by the statement that contradicted her memory. "But did not Asa seek you out first? After he met me outside the synagogue during Shavuot?"

He furrowed his dark brows in confusion. "No. His father and I brokered an agreement years ago. He donated funds toward the new synagogue in exchange for your hand, and therefore my goodwill. He is not a fool, Tikva. He knows that we rabbis hold the ear of the people in this city. His continuing contributions to our coffers are certainly welcome, and we've ensured that his name is held in high regard in this region."

Confusion swirled in Tikva's mind. Asa had told her that he'd been enthralled by her beauty that day and had not rested until his father approached hers to beg for a betrothal. And yet it seemed she had been nothing but a bargaining tool between her father and Nachman instead.

"How fortunate that you've fallen pregnant so soon. It will ensure the connection is strong between us for years to come."

A pang of deep hurt pressed between her ribs. It seemed her father considered the life within her womb as much of a commodity as her own.

Her father smiled as he reached to place a hand atop her head. "I am proud of you, daughter. You have done so well." Then he lifted his voice again, to pray a blessing over her and the child who'd fulfilled his wishes before it had even taken a breath.

Her mother and Helena looked on with undisguised pride as well, both of them just as thrilled as her father that Tikva had done her duty to their respective families.

As the rain pattered hard against the shutters, Tikva prayed once again for Asa to come home, not only to wrap her in his arms and chase away the loneliness but to reassure her that he had chosen her as his wife, that he'd offered for her hand because he cared for her, and not purchased her to ensure security for his trade in Ptolemais.

CHAPTER THREE

There was nothing Helena could say that would keep Tikva inside today. Sunlight had beckoned from the moment of her waking, and she'd slipped out of the house as soon as her mother-in-law had been distracted by an argument between the head cook and one of her charges. It had been a week since she'd been to the bluff, and she meant to spend a long while there today praying over Asa and soaking up the warmth of this fine day, without Mina and Dara trailing behind her. After days of heavy rain that had kept most everyone indoors, the market should be thriving with life, and she was eager to discover which new shipments had arrived.

The port of Ptolemais had been a destination for seafaring trade since ancient times, long before Israel had pushed the Canaanites from the land, but the Romans had transformed it into the busy port it was now—a place where ships docked with goods from all over the world. People with skin in every shade flooded into the city, making Tikva wonder just how far they'd traveled to be here. She wished she could speak the many languages they brought with them so she might ask them questions about their homelands. But as it was, she could only sate her curiosity by examining the myriad items available in the marketplace. Balms, perfumes, fabrics, pottery, wine, and hundreds of other offerings overflowed the stalls, wagon beds, and shops that filled the center of town.

Tikva loved the layers upon layers of voices, foreign and familiar, that vied for attention in the streets, and the happy greetings of the merchants who did the same. Hopefully, today she'd even see a few of her friends. Lilah and Margalit frequented the market on the fourth day of the week, and there was also a chance that other girls she'd grown up with might be there as well, many of them already married and raising children of their own. She was eager to talk about her coming child with other young mothers and ask about things she was embarrassed to discuss with her husband's mother.

Just outside the marketplace, she came across a group of beggars in the shadow of a building. Dressed in threadbare rags, they lifted palms to every passerby, their voices raised in supplication. One man was blind and another had shriveled legs. With them were three women seemingly whole-bodied but hollow-eyed and gaunt, the youngest with an infant at her breast.

One of the women caught her eye and started toward her, hand outstretched. Uneasy, Tikva turned her eyes to the ground as she hurried past, the three coins in the purse around her neck somehow feeling a bit heavier as she lengthened her stride, but she remembered well her father's warning of thieves in places like these. Asa was always generous with regular offerings for distribution to the poor, just as her own father was. If these beggars were truly in need they should go to the priests, not harass people in the streets.

Brushing off the unsettling feeling as she entered into the market, she began to meander through the rows, breathing in the many lovely smells of baked goods and feasting her eyes on the brilliant fabrics and varicolored baskets. Not seeing anyone she knew as she walked, she spent some time chatting with a kind trader and his wife who told tales of their journeys to Egypt and Ethiopia and of men who shimmied up tall trees to pluck ingredients for the unguents they sold. Noticing that the sun was now high in the sky and Helena would undoubtedly be fretting over her absence, Tikva excused herself from the couple and turned to head to the bluff, determined to have at least a few minutes searching the horizon for Asa before she returned home to be chastised.

However, at the very end of the row of stalls, a table stacked with pottery caught her eye. This market was full of jars and bowls and cups made from clay that had been brought in on ships from Athens or Rome, but these were different, more delicately formed than the usual utilitarian vessels. She stopped to admire a tall stoppered jug, glazed in a bluish-green, that stood proudly at the center of the display. It sparkled in the sunlight, as if tiny chips of gold were embedded in its surface. Enthralled, she reached out a finger to trace a glittering swirl down the length of the jug.

"Do you like it?" came a voice, causing Tikva to jerk her hand back. She'd not even noticed the young man sitting on a stool in the shadow of a neighboring building.

"Oh, yes. It is beautiful. I've never seen its like," Tikva answered.

The man gave her a gentle smile, his dark brown eyes echoing the gesture. Something about his face seemed familiar, but Tikva could not place him in her memory. "I'm glad to hear it. It's one of my favorite pieces."

"Where is it from?" she asked. "Egypt?"

"No," he said, with a humble curl of his lips. "It is mine."

"You made this?" She allowed her eyes to trace over the rest of the pottery on the table. Each one was masterful, some glazed to a glassy polish and some painted with flowers or geometric designs. But each was a work of art. On the ground around the table were stacked more useful items: jugs, cups, footbaths, and amphorae, finely crafted but not nearly as lovely. Those displayed on the table were pearls among stones.

She opened her mouth to ask the young man how he'd learned such things but was interrupted by a familiar voice calling her name. She glanced over her shoulder to find her cousin Lilah approaching.

"Tikva, that is you!" said Lilah, arms wide to embrace her. But she halted with a little gasp, and her eyes widened as she looked down at Tikva's middle.

"You are with child?" she asked, her bright smile growing even more brilliant. "How did I not hear of this? How much longer?"

A flush of pleasure rose to Tikva's cheeks, but she dropped her voice so as not to share her private news with the potter. "The midwife believes I have perhaps four months or so left to wait."

"Oh, cousin, I am so pleased for you," said Lilah, her eyes glittering. Lilah had always been the merriest of their group of friends, always quick with a smile and jest. "Asa must be thrilled."

"He does not yet know," said Tikva. "He's been to sea for nearly five months now."

"Do you expect him soon?"

"Any day." Tikva glanced northward toward the bluff, another wave of longing for Asa washing over her. To distract herself from the thought, she turned back to the table of pottery. "Have you seen this man's work, Lilah? Isn't it extraordinary?"

Her cousin lifted her eyes to the potter still sitting on the stool, a tight smile in place. "Yes. I have. It is lovely." For someone as cheerful as Lilah, her stilted tone struck Tikva as quite odd.

"*Shalom,*" she said with a nod. "How is your wife?" Her seeming acquaintance with the potter and his wife surprised Tikva, but perhaps Lilah had met him in the market before.

"She is well," responded the potter. "Resting, which is why I am tending the stall today."

"Her time is soon?" asked Lilah.

"Perhaps only a few days more," he said. The excitement evident in the brightening of his countenance made it clear that his wife was soon to give birth to his child.

Lilah nodded. "Many blessings to you both," she said with a dismissive air before turning back to Tikva. "Margalit and I miss you. Please do come for a visit this week. Since you've been married and now live across town, we barely see you anymore. All the girls have been asking after you, in fact. They will be thrilled to know that you are with child. You must come and share your news."

"I will. If anything to escape Asa's mother and her constant hovering. I think she fears I might break in two at any moment in my condition."

Lilah laughed and kissed Tikva's cheek. "I must go. I told my mother I'd purchase some of her favorite sheep's-milk cheese and a few pomegranates and then come right home. I am sure she is wondering what has happened to me."

Her cousin swept away, leaving Tikva frowning at her back in confusion. She'd never known Lilah to cut short any conversation. What had made her so ill at ease?

"If you like that jug, then this piece may interest you as well." The potter's voice jarred her from pondering Lilah's strange behavior. The man was now standing just on the other side of the table, holding out a blue-green vase, the lip fluted and curled with fascinating delicacy. When Tikva lowered her eyes to the hand wrapped about its narrow neck, the reason for Lilah's uneasiness became all too apparent.

The last two fingers of the man's hands were shorter than the rest and his wrist was curved ever-so-slightly in an unnatural fashion. She knew that hand. Her eyes dropped to his side where a crutch was tucked beneath his arm and where she now realized his painfully twisted foot was hidden behind the stand of goods.

Of course. This was Simcha, a boy she remembered well from her childhood. She'd seen him many times over the years, hobbling through the streets of Ptolemais. The youngest son of the local potter, Simcha had spent most of his time here in the market, aiding his father. But once in a while she'd seen him watching her friends play together, a look of longing in the gaze he directed at their games of chase, ball-kicking, or wooden sword battles.

A few years ago, he seemed to disappear altogether, which is why she'd not seen him grow into the man who now stood before her. Where had he gone? She'd not heard that he'd married, although who would have thought to tell her such a thing? Strange that Lilah even knew about his wife at all, especially since her attitude toward the man was so cold.

The feeling of uneasiness from her run-in with the beggars returned. Simcha seemed like a kind man. She even remembered him smiling at her from afar when they were children, but she did not know what to say to a man who, for as long as she remembered, lived on the fringes of the town in one of the mud-brick hovels that more often than not housed large, extended families in one or two rooms. From the number of pottery stalls she'd passed in her wanderings today, Simcha's business looked to be suffering from the extensive trade in the area. And yet, seeing the skill with which he created his goods, she wondered why she seemed to be the only customer at his stall. Was everyone as put off by his deformities as her cousin seemed to be?

Realizing that she'd hesitated too long, and he was looking at her with a hint of curiosity, she accepted the vase from Simcha and studied its mottled surface, her fingertips tracing the cascade of green and blue as it swirled around the vase like a storm cloud. "It's extraordinary," she whispered. "How did you learn to do such a thing?"

"I traveled to Egypt," he said. "I lived in Alexandria for a few years with my mother's family. My uncles taught me this technique."

"Alexandria? That's where you disappeared to?" Tikva asked. His brows lifted in surprise. "You noticed my absence?"

"I—I did not see you in the market with your father anymore."

He smiled at her again, and she was surprised by the kindness in his expression, especially since she'd never bothered to speak to him over the years. And also, since she'd kept her distance, she'd never realized that he was fairly handsome, with rich, mahogany-colored hair and deep brown eyes. She wondered whom he'd married. Perhaps she was someone he'd met in Egypt, a woman who'd looked past the deformity and saw the man.

Again she heard her name called out and turned to ascertain the source. She saw one of Helena's servant girls scurrying toward her, wide-eyed and panic stricken.

"Tikva! You must return to the house," said Mina. "Helena needs you."

"What is wrong?" Tikva asked, her heart quavering with fear. "Is she ill?"

"No." Mina wrung her hands together, her gaze flitting to Simcha and then back to Tikva. "Please, just come with me now." There were tears in the girl's eyes. She'd never seen a servant so overwrought.

Tikva's hands began to shake. "Mina. You must tell me what has happened."

"I cannot, mistress. Helena said I must retrieve you. She will—"

"Tell me now."

Mina flinched at the uncharacteristically sharp command, her eyes on the ground. "The ship...your husband and his father were on..." She cleared her throat, and tears shimmered in her eyes. "It went down off the coast of Tyre in the storms. Only two sailors survived to bring word. I'm so sorry—"

The moment the vase crashed to the ground, shattering into a hundred pieces, Tikva's mind went blank, as if stuffed with only heavy black wool and the throbbing pulse in her head that smothered the sound of Mina's words. Her eyes flittered open and shut, blackness to blue sky, again and again. Arms encircled her as she lay on the ground, a deep voice uttering something she could not comprehend over the pain that suddenly gripped her lower back and abdomen. Agony ripped and tore at her body until darkness swallowed the heavens.

PART II

CHAPTER FOUR

◆

Twelve years later

Tikva startled awake but refused to open her eyes, still grasping at the last precious threads of unconsciousness. Hands on her belly, she searched for the swollen curve that she'd brushed over only moments ago in her dream, along with the flicker of life that, for at least a short time, had felt so close, so real.

But the slope of her stomach was not rounded, the sweetly mounded flesh no longer growing day by day, stretching to accommodate the joy building beneath her heart. Instead, her palms met only with sharply jutting hipbones and an abdomen that lay flat. Empty. Dead. Just like she was.

Knowing she could prolong the moment no longer, for Helena always masterfully gauged Tikva's awareness within her first breaths outside of sleep, she allowed her eyelids to slide open and latched her gaze upon the crumbling ceiling. Helena immediately shifted on her own pallet nearby, as if she'd been simply waiting for Tikva to awaken before stirring. Tikva flexed her icy toes, her warm woolen blanket having abandoned her feet in the night, and she wondered whether she'd kept her mother-in-law from sleep with her restlessness. Helena had never complained of such a thing, but many were the mornings that the blanket was either twisted like a piece of woolen yarn or was halfway on the dirt floor instead of on Tikva's body. She guessed that there were times she thrashed and called out during one of her nightmares.

It was always the same dream. The waves. Gasping for breath. Pain. Darkness. And then the high, piercing wail of a newborn babe. Yet no matter how many times she traveled to that hazy story in her mind, still she awoke to the same crumbling ceiling and the same flat belly.

"We must awaken, daughter," said Helena as she twisted to leave her own cocoon of blankets.

With a shiver Tikva sat up, pulling her frozen feet under the wool and sliding her stiff fingers under her thighs, hoping to thaw them.

"Get up, girl." Helena clapped her hands with each word, her clipped tones far too loud for the still morning. "If you move, your body will warm itself."

It did not matter that Helena no longer had an entire household to run. She managed Tikva with as much efficiency as she had her servants, and Tikva knew better than to argue. And since Simcha had most generously offered the two of them work when they'd become destitute a few months after Asa and Nachman died, she refused to let him down either.

Tikva pulled herself off the meager pallet and moved to wash her hands and face in her pot beneath the sole window in their tiny one-room abode. The memory of an alabaster washing basin filled with steaming water by a maidservant and scented with hyacinth and rosemary flittered by, but she would not dwell on it. The years had made her adept at sweeping such longing thoughts back into the clouds where they belonged.

Giving Tikva privacy to tend to her needs and change her soiled rags, as she always did, Helena turned her back to prepare a small meal to take with them to the market. With the familiarity born of thousands of repetitions, Tikva rinsed her bloodied rags in a separate pot of water and then laid them out to dry atop a flat stone she kept beneath the window for that purpose.

Her baby's life might have been stolen on that one, awful day, but Tikva's had been seeping from her body, moment by moment, for twelve eternal years.

Even so, her husband's mother, still caught in the throes of her own grief over the loss of her husband and her only son, had refused to let her waste to nothing after she'd lost the last piece of Asa. She'd insisted that Tikva eat. Insisted that she dress and wash her body. Insisted that she leave the house and brave the sun, even if the people of the city disdained her for doing so.

And even after the two of them had been driven from that lovely, whitewashed villa near the center of town, with its smooth tile floors and soft ocean breezes, and into this disintegrating hovel at the very edge of the city, Helena had refused to let Tikva curl into herself.

Pulling her veil low over her eyes and tight over her face, a feeble attempt at anonymity, Tikva allowed Helena to lead her out of the room they'd dwelt in for the past eight years, into the narrow alley and toward Simcha's workshop.

Since the sun had barely made an appearance on the eastern horizon, few neighbors were yet stirring. Those that were outside already, women tending to animals or heading toward the well to gather water, offered "shalom" to Helena as they passed. And yet few offered the same to Tikva, most allowing their glances to bounce away from her eyes or turning their heads without so much as a smile.

However, she was used to ignoring the slight and did not fault them. She was *tameh*—an unclean woman afflicted for the past twelve years with constant bleeding after her child had been ripped from her womb. Nothing could ever make her clean again. And nothing could make the people of Ptolemais forget that to touch her meant impurity, nor wash away the accusing looks of those who considered her affliction a just punishment for some sin she'd committed.

The two women continued onto the trade road that led to where Simcha lived and crafted his pottery, a place even farther from Ptolemais than their own cluster of ramshackle dwellings and where the constant smoke and acrid smell of the outdoor kiln would not disturb neighbors.

A small group of beggars shambled by Tikva and Helena, heading toward the city. Of course, those that she'd scurried by on her way to enjoy the wonders of the market twelve years ago were long gone, replaced by an ever-changing flock of the lame, the blind, the impoverished widows, the orphans, and the lepers.

And just as Tikva did every time she came in contact with one of these desperate souls, she thanked Adonai for the mother-in-law who had not abandoned her when both of their husbands had perished in the sea and left a business behind that was all too soon swallowed by debt. For, if not for Helena, she, too, would have been on a corner years ago, palm up, pleading with strangers for the smallest of coins to still the grinding beast in her belly. No—without Helena she would have been dead long ago.

◆

Tikva knelt beside the handcart, examining the wheel that had wobbled all the way from Simcha's home into the market, threatening to spill the delicate wares along the way. She hoped the ancient contraption would make it back to the workshop and she'd not be left with a useless pile of wood in the middle of the road.

"*She* hasn't handled these, has she?" came the voice of a female customer at the stall behind her. "I have no interest in unclean goods."

Even without looking back at Helena, Tikva could practically feel her mother-in-law bristle. "No," she responded in a low, smooth voice that anyone who knew her well would recognize as dangerous. "Tikva is careful to observe the Law. She pushes the cart back and forth between the potter's workshop but does not touch the wares themselves."

Tikva's body curved forward as her belly contracted, an instinctive response to not only the personal attack but also her guilt that Helena was forced to repeat such things whenever she was present in the market. Which meant that after her second trip with the handcart to stock the stall every morning, Tikva immediately returned to the workshop to aid Simcha, leaving Helena to barter with customers unimpeded.

Still in a kneeling position, Tikva pretended to fuss with the loose wheel while waiting for the transaction to be completed. However, Helena responded to the woman's inquiry about whatever piece had caught her fancy with a price twice as high as Tikva knew it to be worth and then refused to lower the value even one tiny bronze mite.

The customer left in a huff, with a threat to patronize their competition instead. Helena, to her credit, did not raise her voice to the rude woman but instead offered directions to the shop of Medad, the trader whose cheap, imported goods were famous for cracking within days of purchase.

"You did not have to do that, Helena," Tikva said as she pushed herself to standing and brushed the dust from her knees.

Helena made a noise of annoyance as she carefully set the turquoise vase back among Simcha's other lovely creations. "Simcha has made only a few with such a brilliant color. She did not deserve to own such a rare and beautiful thing."

"She only desires to follow the Law," said Tikva. "You know that anything I touch becomes unclean. You should not turn away money."

"Perhaps," said her mother-in-law with a sniff. "But kindness is worth much more than shekels."

"Neither we, nor Simcha and Adina, can fill our bellies with kindness, Helena. Please, don't let them suffer on my account. We need every sale possible."

Helena folded her arms over her chest, the stubborn set of her jaw challenging Tikva's admonition. But finally she loosened her stance and sighed. "You are right. I should not have lost my temper, but I do not like to see you abused for something that is in no way your fault."

With a surge of gratitude, Tikva wished she could publicly embrace her mother-in-law. Although they'd barely known each other before Asa died, the woman had offered abundant compassion and unconditional friendship over the past twelve years, regardless of the way the rest of the town looked upon her for doing so—something Tikva's own family refused to do. Tears sprang to her eyes, so she cleared her throat and blinked them away.

"I'd best return to the workshop and help prepare the days' clay for Simcha," Tikva said. "But if you need me, please send a messenger."

"Go on," Helena said. "And don't forget to take along that basket I prepared. There are a few dates in there for Adina, along with some fresh olive oil that came in on the ship from Cyprus. She told me their supply was getting low."

With an obedient nod, Tikva fetched the basket and nestled it into the straw bedding of the pushcart, as always astounded by the generosity of the woman whom she'd once feared but who had now come to replace her own mother in many ways. With a grunt of exertion, she lifted the handles of the two-wheeled cart and urged it forward, praying that the wobbly wheel, along with her own meager strength, would last to the end of the second of her four daily journeys between the market and the potter's house.

CHAPTER FIVE

❖

By some miracle, the handcart survived the journey to Simcha's home, in spite of how many times Tikva was forced to stop and rest along the way. Gone were her fleet-footed days, when she'd gone nearly mad being penned up inside Helena's grand whitewashed home. Day by day, moment by moment, her youth had been drained from her body, along with her lifeblood. Now every single activity stole her breath and took twice as long to accomplish as before. Even walking down a flat road winded her, and four trips to the market each day was nearly enough to flatten her.

But she refused to complain. Simcha would likely give anything to have the ability to push that rickety cart along the pitted dirt road to Ptolemais, and she and Helena owed him so much for his kindnesses, a debt they would never be able to repay.

The smoke from Simcha's kiln greeted her first, making her nose twitch against its acrid odor. She followed the familiar smell around the side of the two-room house he and Adina called home to the open-air workshop his grandfather had constructed many years before. It too was showing its age, the wood weathered and splintering. A few stones from the foundation had shifted from their moorings, and the tall clay kiln at the center was liberally painted with soot and bedecked with cracks.

The Healer's Touch: Tikva's Story

With the glow of the flame lighting his face, Simcha bent to place one of the pots he'd made yesterday inside the kiln. He would spend much of his day adjusting the heat within the oven, ensuring that each piece was fired for the correct amount of time within its belly.

Sometimes Simcha would carefully remove a pot or bowl from the heat, apply a glaze or wash over the paint, and then return the piece to the fire, a process to strengthen the clay vessel without destroying the delicate decorations he'd painstakingly applied. He'd picked up such advanced techniques during his years in Alexandria, where he'd been sent to learn his trade, only returning to take over the business when his mother died and his elderly father was nearing the end of his own life.

The fact that very few people understood the extraordinary skill it took to create such beautiful work and regularly undercut its worth made both Tikva and Helena resentful. Where the people of Ptolemais regarded Tikva as something unclean, they saw Simcha as little more than the product of a curse, or even some sin committed by his parents. Therefore, Simcha continued to struggle for his daily bread, no matter that the vessels he crafted were by far the best in the market.

Tikva waited until he was clear of the fiery kiln before approaching. "The handcart will need repair before I return to the market to bring back the goods."

"I thought as much," he said. "I told you I would fix it before you left. I imagine it was a difficult journey back and forth today."

Tikva offered a tight smile. She should have waited, it was true, but she'd been anxious to deliver the pots to Helena and return. She abhorred the dank little room they lived in and feared hurtful interactions in the marketplace, but here at Simcha's workshop she was able to keep her hands busy, to keep her mind occupied with assisting him, and if she was truly honest with herself, she felt more at peace here than she had anywhere else for the past twelve years.

Balancing on his crutch with the expertise of a man who'd long ago adapted to the limitations of his twisted foot, Simcha selected three plates he'd made yesterday and laid them inside the kiln as well. "Go inside and rest while I deal with the cart. Adina was worried about you. I nearly had to tie her down to keep her from running down to the market to make sure you were well."

A smile curved Tikva's lips. Adina likely had driven Simcha to distraction with her worries. Thankfully, he was the most patient of men and would no more raise his voice to her than he would cut off his good hand. "Helena sent some dates and olive oil to her. I'll take them in and then begin treading that clay."

"Tikva." Simcha's tone was the nearest to sharpness she'd ever heard. "The clay can wait. I still have some from the last batch that is useable. You look weary. Go, rest."

She nodded, chastened by the strangely terse way in which he'd spoken, and turned to make her way into the house, eyes burning with a sudden wash of tears.

"Wait," he said.

Tikva halted but did not turn to face him.

"Forgive me for snapping at you. I did not mean to—" He sighed. "I am only concerned, Tikva. You look so pale this morning. So tired."

I am tired, she thought. *I am so weary that one day my bones will fold in upon themselves. In fact, weariness has consumed me so thoroughly, body and soul, that there are days I wish I had been buried with my babe in my arms.*

"I am fine," she replied and left the workshop, avoiding yet another discussion with Simcha about her growing fatigue. She knew she was fading. Her skin had become as colorless as linen left in the sun, her hands and feet were perpetually the temperature of ice even when standing near Simcha's kiln, and she'd long ago adapted to the constant soreness in her mouth and muscles.

She was also tired of Helena and Simcha hovering over her and the way they glanced at each other with obvious concern when they thought she was not looking. It was more than likely that she would not live much longer. She could feel the end advancing on her like a Roman legion in full regalia, but she would work until the end, doing her very best to repay both of them for their generosity to a woman whom others treated like refuse.

Adina met her at the door, smile wide and wild black curls framing her small face. "You're here!" she said before throwing her arms about Tikva. "Abba would not let me go find you. I wanted to help you push the cart."

Tikva laid a palm on the girl's cheek. "Thank you, precious one. I am well. I've brought you some dates from Helena."

A squeal of pleasure emanated from the twelve-year-old's lips as Tikva handed her the basket sent by Helena, washing away the last of the sadness that thoughts of her oncoming demise had wrought. Although, truly, Tikva was very rarely able to dwell on anything but the sweetness and vibrant spirit of Simcha's daughter whenever she was in the girl's presence.

However, it had taken years for the sharp ache to lessen. Years for her to savor embraces from the beautiful child who, in spite of having lost her mother at only a few months old, was a brilliant light to all around her. Sometimes she still searched the girl's face and wondered what her own baby might have looked like had he taken a breath in this world. And watching Simcha interact with his daughter always reminded her that Asa had not even known she'd been pregnant when he perished at sea.

Taking her by the hand, Adina led Tikva to a chair, insisting that she sit down, and then regaled her with a story about two neighbor boys who'd thrown dirt in her hair when she'd been milking the goat out front. Tikva laughed when Adina explained how, instead of responding to the little miscreants, she'd lifted her chin like a queen and ignored them until they gave up and ran off to find someone else to pester.

"Very wise," said Tikva. "If you'd lost your head at their provocation, they would have counted it a victory and continued their attack." Having endured this same situation many times over the past few years, she hoped Adina would take the lesson to heart.

Many were the children who taunted Tikva in the street, calling out her uncleanness to bystanders, or even naming her a *chazir*, for many regarded her as little more than a sow in the mud and just as abominable. Of course, these young ones had learned such things from their parents, whose weapons of choice were more subtle to be sure, but cruelty begets cruelty.

Adina regarded her silently for a few moments, her brown eyes full of some ambiguous emotion, and Tikva wondered if there had been others who teased her, perhaps had mocked her father's odd gait or twisted hand.

"I wish you did not have to go back and forth to your home every day," Adina said. "I wish you lived here with us instead."

The innocent comment curled around Tikva's heart and squeezed, but she smiled to hide the ache. "I could not leave Helena all alone, now could I? She'd be so lonely."

"We have room for both of you here. We have the upper room where my grandfather used to sleep," Adina said, her eyes alighting with hope as she considered the possibilities. "There is no reason for you both to live so far away when we could all share."

Tikva allowed her gaze to travel around the room, taking in the sparse furnishings and the small mud-brick oven in the corner, the place that had once been the domain of Simcha's wife. Although Tikva had never met Rachel, somehow her presence still lingered. What Adina had no way of knowing was that the decision whether or not to live in this house had been made long ago.

The girl had been only six months of age when her mother died, thanks to a fever that swept through the marketplace with fury and cut down nearly a third of the merchants—most likely some illness that had been imported along with goods from across the sea. Around the same time, Helena and Tikva had been forced to sell what was left of their belongings and move from their lovely home.

Within only a few weeks Simcha, although still in the depths of grief, came to Helena and Tikva with a proposal—Tikva could marry him, help him with his motherless daughter and his pottery business, and the two women could come live in this home.

At first Tikva had been horrified. Why would a man she barely knew suggest such a thing? And yet he'd been so gracious in the asking, stating again and again that he'd considered how they might all lean on one another after death had stolen so much. And truly it would have been the best solution if Tikva had not been still bleeding with no explanation from any of the physicians or midwives Helena had summoned in those early months.

Even so, Helena had encouraged her to accept Simcha, to take hold of the security such an arrangement would offer. But, for the first and last time, Tikva stood firm against her mother-in-law, refusing to even consider such a thing because Simcha deserved more than a woman he could not even touch and whose womb would never bear another child.

Thankfully, he had not pressed his suit but returned again a few days later suggesting that if she was uncomfortable with a marriage, the three of them could partner in his business. Without his wife, who'd manned the stall in the market and assisted with preparing the clay, he was at a loss as to how to continue his work. And with the addition of an infant whom he would be forced to tend alone, since his parents were dead and none of the rest of his family remained in the city, he had no way to keep afloat.

No matter her misgivings, the desperation in his voice had convinced Tikva that, if anything, she and Helena could help Simcha provide for his daughter—even though in those early days the sight of Adina's tiny body and the sound of her hungry cries had gutted her.

"We do well as we are, don't you think?" Tikva asked, standing to press a kiss to the top of Adina's head and hoping she would not push the issue any further. "Now, let us go help your father. There is clay to tread before I head back with the cart this afternoon to collect whatever goods Helena has not sold."

Thankfully, the prospect of squishing her naked toes into the slurry of dirt and water distracted Adina from more talk of her futile wishes. She bolted through the door, calling out an affectionate greeting to her father, all thoughts of Tikva and Helena joining their household forgotten for the moment.

For as much as Tikva adored Simcha's daughter and respected the man himself, nothing had changed over the last twelve years. She was still untouchable, and this home, along with the peace and security that resided within, would never be hers.

CHAPTER SIX

✦

"I do not understand why you insist on going," Helena had said as Tikva pulled a wooden wide-tooth comb through her hair. "All it does is hurt you."

"I have not gone in nearly a month. It feels…" Tikva tapped the comb against her lips. "It feels wrong to avoid the synagogue on Shabbat. My father—"

A burst of air flew through Helena's lips, cutting off her justification. "Is the prince of hypocrites."

Tikva flinched as she reached for the less threadbare of her two head scarves to layer over her hair.

"Forgive me," said Helena, brushing aside Tikva's hands to finish the job of tucking in a few stray locks beneath the brown wool. "I should not have said such a thing, no matter how I feel about the way your family has treated you." She grasped Tikva's face in both hands and looked into her eyes. "But must you go and torture yourself? No one will be the wiser if you stay here with me."

"Come with me," Tikva pleaded, gripping Helena's hand. "It is a beautiful day, and I am feeling stronger now than I have in a month."

After a long pause, in which Tikva nearly allowed herself to hope, her mother-in-law shook her head, jaw set like stone.

"I went to that synagogue every Shabbat while my Nachman was alive. I took his God as my own when we married, turned my back on the ones I knew in my homeland. You know this, daughter. But that vow is on the bottom of the sea, along with my husband and my son. Unless Adonai raises the dead to life, that is where it will stay."

They'd had the same conversation on many a Shabbat over the years. Each time Tikva knew her words were futile, and each time Helena made it clear how frustrated she was that Tikva continued to make the journey into town just to sit alone outside a building. But the years of training in the ways of Torah were too much ingrained in Tikva. No matter that she was no longer allowed to set foot inside, she felt the compulsion to go, to sit in the shadow of the beautiful synagogue at the center of Ptolemais where the people of Adonai lifted up praises to the Most High and the words of Moses were read aloud.

❖

Tikva leaned her back against the stone, settling in to await the uplifted voice of the rabbi, the signal that the service inside the synagogue had begun, and wishing that the conversation with her mother-in-law had, for once, gone a different way this morning.

As the Shema began and the people of Israel were called to hear and obey the One True God who'd rescued their ancestors from Egypt, Tikva closed her eyes and allowed the beauty of the words to wash over her. The familiarity sparked memories of sitting beside her mother as her father fulfilled his rabbinical duties, and the pride she'd felt as he lifted blessings over the people. Even now, her ears searched out the rich voice she'd once adored, wondering whether he would be the one to read the words of the Torah today. She still remembered the rumble deep in his chest as she sat on his lap as a small girl and the comfort she'd felt in his arms. In spite of everything, she missed his voice.

Why, Adonai? cried her heart, spilling over with grief. *What did I do to cause You to cut me from my family's embrace?* For no matter how much Helena had insisted over the years that Tikva was not to blame for this affliction, that some sin she'd harbored had not instigated the loss of her child and her health, the never-ending cycle of shame and guilt remained.

After the righteous words were read, by someone other than her father, and the last echo of worship dissipated into the blue sky, Tikva wiped tears from her cheeks, unfolded her weary body, and stood to brush the dust from her tunic. With a jolt, she realized people were already leaving the building, so she skittered over to hide behind a cluster of trees to watch the flow of bodies from the ornately decorated synagogue that her own marriage helped fund.

She held her breath as she scanned the crowd, eager for a glimpse of her family and hoping no one would recognize her beneath her double veil. Her greedy eyes devoured the sight of three of her four brothers emerging, deep in conversation. Although none of them had spoken to her in years, she still held cherished memories of playing together in the courtyard behind their home, of chilly nights curled up like puppies together on a shared pallet, and their collective thrill of anticipation as they discussed upcoming festival celebrations. And yet the boys who'd guarded her like centurions when they were children, who'd taken their office as brothers and protectors with the sincerity of a sacred vow, refused now to sully themselves by even looking her way. They had to know she came here, since it had been her habit all this time. But they walked on, heads not turning. Their wives, two of whom she'd never met, followed close by without sparing a glance her way.

Helena's question as to why she tortured herself in this way floated to her mind, and for the thousandth time she asked herself the same. Why did she continue to prod at this wound? The answer came back as it always did. Because she couldn't stop. Even just the small glimpses of her family reminded her that once she'd been the daughter who'd walked among them. Once she'd been the girl all the others vied to sit beside and whisper secrets to. Once she'd been the bride desired by a handsome man whose pursuit had made the other maidens envious. It reminded her that she'd not always been this way, an outcast, her name such a reproach that to most she was known only as the bleeding woman of Ptolemais.

Her mother emerged from the doors of the synagogue, a smile on her face as she lifted it, as if welcoming the sun. Her friend Tamar walked alongside her, chattering like a sparrow as she'd done for as long as Tikva could remember. In fact, without a doubt, it was Tamar who'd spread the word of Tikva's affliction from the very start.

Tikva held her breath, slipping her body from behind the cluster of cyprus trees. Hoping. Praying.

Her mother's eyes lifted, snagging on Tikva's gaze in recognition, then traveled down her body, an expression of curiosity quickly melting into despair. Then she snapped her attention back up to Tikva's face, the intensity burning Tikva's skin. Fear flashed in her mother's eyes, and she took a step forward, her lips parting as if to say something. But in the same moment, Tamar noticed the direction of her gaze and looped her arm around her friend's elbow, effectively locking her in place as the two halted in the street. Tamar leaned over to whisper something in her mother's ear and gestured back toward the synagogue.

Tamar had been there the day Tikva had revealed her affliction to her mother, after she'd bled for weeks without ceasing and came to plead for advice on what to do when none of the midwives' remedies worked. And it had been Tamar who reminded her mother in that moment that Tikva's presence in her home would be cause for rumor and censure from the people of Ptolemais and that it would be best for Tikva to not return until her body was whole and pure.

Tikva's heart pounded as she watched her mother's silent struggle, the constant beat a steady *please, please, please* against her ribs. But even as she kept her eyes latched to Tikva's, her mother's shoulders sagged. It was like it had always been. Tikva could feel the love vibrating across the plaza and knew that her mother wanted nothing more than to shake off Tamar and fly to her daughter's side. It was the only reason Tikva continued to come here, to see the remnants of the affection her mother held for her in her eyes. It was torture, yes, but it was something, a few drops of mother-love in a sea of emptiness.

With apology and grief in her eyes, Tikva's mother turned away, tripping along obediently behind Tamar. But just before the two women turned the corner to head toward the place Tikva had once called home, her mother glanced over her shoulder and wiped a tear from her cheek.

A sob rose in Tikva's throat, and tears she'd not allowed herself to indulge in for many years burned behind her eyes. She turned to flee, vision blurred, but before she'd managed to take more than five half-blind steps toward home, she slammed into someone's broad back. Blinking the errant tears from her eyes, she mumbled an apology and skittered backward. Whomever she'd plowed into was a rabbi, his embellished robes and long *tzitzit* making it clear that he was a well-respected Pharisee. He would, without a doubt, be furious that an unclean woman had dared touch him.

But it was not an unknown rabbi who turned to glare down at her. It was her father, who was surrounded by a group of his fellow teachers of the Law.

His beard was fully gray, a startling contrast from the rich brown it had once been, back when Tikva entertained herself in the evenings by winding her little-girl fingers into the wiry curls at his jaw. But instead of the adoring affection that had once emanated from his light brown eyes—ones that matched her own—there was nothing but the detached perusal of a stranger. His lips pressed into a sharp frown as he swept his gaze from her head to her feet, a gaze that communicated unmitigated disgust with the bedraggled, emaciated form before him. Then he spun away without a word, his overlong blue-knotted tzitzit flaring in wide arcs as he did so, his stride long and purposeful as he separated himself from the girl he'd once called his precious little flower. And Tikva knew in that moment that she would not come within fifty paces of this synagogue, or her family, ever again.

CHAPTER SEVEN

✧

"I want to speak with you about something, Tikva," said Helena as they were preparing for bed.

"What is it?" asked Tikva, trying once again to lift her weary arms to the task of braiding her hair. Her throbbing fingers attempted to wrangle the curls for a few moments, but when she'd created nothing but a knotted mess, they slipped back to her lap, defeated. She'd deal with the tangles in the morning. Since the day she'd run into her family at the synagogue three weeks ago, her body had seemed even more sapped of energy.

"Here," said her mother-in-law, settling in behind Tikva on the pallet and swiping hair back from her face. "Let me."

Too tired to pull away, Tikva allowed her mother-in-law to braid her hair, hoping that the woman would not see the moisture that gathered in her eyes—both for the memories of her own mother doing the same thing years before, and for the feeling of someone, anyone, touching her without flinching away as if she were a monster.

"There is a new physician in Caesarea. A lauded man from Greece who is rumored to have come to Israel to establish a place of healing in the same vein as the famous one in Epidaurus," said Helena.

"I had my fill of physicians, Helena. You know this."

It had been years since Helena had even broached the subject of medicine to treat Tikva's affliction. Not only because they no longer had money to waste on such things, but after months of Helena dragging her to every physician, every midwife, and every self-proclaimed healer in the region, Tikva had refused to see another one.

Every humiliating exam she'd endured, every stomach-churning herbal potion she'd swallowed, and every time she'd been forced to describe the consistency and volume of the blood her body expelled had nicked away at her dignity, until there was little left to guard. But thankfully once she'd been forced to sell her home and all her belongings, Helena no longer had any funds with which to pay for futile medicines or grim-faced physicians with no solutions. It had been ten years since Helena had even bothered to broach the subject.

"But this man is not just any physician, Tikva. He is a student of the school of Hippocrates. He has treated many high-ranking government officials over the past few years. It is said he brought Caesar's favorite nephew back from the brink of death."

"All the physicians you took me to and all the midwives who visited my sickbed had some claim to fame or another, Helena. My condition is not reversible. And even if I were willing to go to some physician, which I am not, we have nothing to pay the man with."

Finished with the braid, Helena slipped around to face Tikva on the pallet and then took her cheeks in her hands, her blue eyes as intense as Tikva had ever seen them.

"You are dying, sweet girl. I can see every one of your ribs. Your spine pokes through your skin, which is as thin as worn papyrus, and you move more like an older woman than I do."

Tikva shrugged, knowing that everything Helena said was true. For many years the blood that stained her rags each morning was little more than a few dark spots, enough to keep her unclean but not enough to soak through. But just after she'd run into her family at the synagogue three weeks ago, the flow had strengthened again.

"You are giving up, aren't you?" Helena's hands dropped to her lap. "You want to leave me."

Tikva sighed. "I don't want any of this. I wanted my baby. I wanted Asa to live. But Adonai took it all. I cannot fight His will. When I die, I die."

"So you will throw away any chance at life? You will leave me without a daughter? Leave Adina without a mother?"

"I am not Adina's mother," Tikva said.

"You are as good as one," said Helena. "It is you who dressed her and fed her and comforted her whenever she was ill when she was small. It is to you she comes to discuss her fears and proclaim her joys. You may not have agreed to Simcha's proposal of marriage, but even so, you have become a mother to his child, whether you meant to or not."

Pain struck Tikva's chest. Had she taken on that role without even realizing it? Did Adina look to her as a replacement for her own mother even though Tikva had not encouraged her to do so? Would Adina grieve Tikva in a way she'd not even known to do for the woman who'd given her life?

"Even if I had any hope that your Greek physician could do anything for me, which I do not, we have no money left, Helena. We have barely enough to lift bread to our mouths, let alone toss at futile promise of miracles."

"I lied," said Helena, her gaze dropping to examine her calloused palms.

"About what?"

"I saved a portion of your dowry," she said. "I knew there would be a day when I was gone, and I could not bear for you to be destitute."

"But how? We sold everything to pay Nachman and Asa's debts. There was nothing left over."

"Nachman kept a bag of coins and three gold rings from your dowry in a secret place beneath the house. He had no more need of it, and I wanted you to be provided for."

"But we could have used that money over the past twelve years or used it to pay Simcha back for his help."

"By the time I discovered it, a few days before we moved from the villa, Simcha had already approached us with his idea of us helping with his business. I knew we would be provided for, if only in a meager way. So I kept it hidden." She pointed up to the ceiling. "It's yours, Tikva. It's tucked up there above the support beam where the mud has worn away. I wasn't planning to tell you until I was near my own end, but this is the time. This physician is the answer, daughter. He can save you, I just know it."

The revelation that Helena had hidden a bag of riches above their heads for years, along with the realization that

Adina considered Tikva a mother, was too much to wrap her mind around.

"I cannot talk about this anymore tonight," said Tikva. "I am far beyond tired."

"Of course," said Helena, sliding over to allow Tikva to nestle beneath her blanket. "But please, consider appealing to this physician. If not for yourself, then for Adina and me. And even for Simcha, who needs your help with his business and his child."

After Helena blew out the oil lamp and settled into her own bed, Tikva's eyes searched the blackness above her, considering the money Helena had hidden up there.

She was going to die. Soon. There was nothing that could be done to save her useless body. But those coins could save Adina from the pinch of hunger in case something happened to Simcha's business after Tikva was gone, or perhaps even provide the girl with her own dowry someday. So for now they would stay where they were, ready to be passed on to Adina when Tikva's time came.

CHAPTER EIGHT

✧

Holding Adina's foot, Tikva dipped a clay cup in the shallow stream and poured another portion of clean water over the girl's muddy toes.

"That tickles!" Adina said, squirming on the rock she was seated upon as Tikva scrubbed her sole with a handful of sand, her giggles reminiscent of when she'd been just a tiny thing on Tikva's lap.

"This won't come off without a bit of work," Tikva said, gripping the girl's heel tighter as Adina tried to wiggle out of her hold. Her own skin was encrusted with dried muck to the middle of her calves, since the two of them had spent the afternoon purifying, mixing, and treading a large batch of clay for Simcha's use.

Tikva dropped Adina's foot back into the water. "Walk out a little farther and soak them so we don't have to scrub so hard."

Adina obeyed, striding out to the middle of the stream with her tunic lifted above her knees. Tikva noticed that the girl's legs had lengthened considerably in the past few months, and gentle curves had begun to form. It would only be another year before Adina would be counted as a woman herself. How had time collapsed on itself so quickly? A wave of sadness washed over Tikva as she remembered that the tiny son who'd never taken a breath would also have been counted a man next year. Instead, he would never see a thirteenth year. He would never marry. Never have children of his own to continue the family legacy. Tikva's failure to give him life had been the ending of Asa's line.

"Do you remember my mother?" Adina asked.

Startled by the question, Tikva tripped back a step, slamming her heel against a sharp rock and wincing at the pain that shot up her leg.

For as many questions as Adina asked over the years, this was the first time she'd asked specifically about her mother. "No, I'm sorry. I wish I did. From what I've heard she was a lovely woman, but we never met."

Adina's large brown eyes were still trained expectantly on her, likely desperate for information about the woman who'd given birth to her within days of Tikva's own tragedy. Tikva searched her memory for any secondhand tidbit she had to offer, coming up with little. The only thing she knew for certain was that the marriage between Simcha and Rachel had been arranged by his uncle back in Alexandria, since Helena had told her this years ago.

"I've been told that she was generous, always bringing meals to neighbors. You inherited her skill for cooking, without a doubt." The compliment made the girl smile, since she did love to help Helena and Tikva prepare meals and especially adored making sweet treats for her father. "And it is plain to see that she was beautiful, just by looking at you." Tikva brushed a palm over the girl's sweetly rounded cheek. It would not be long before the boys in town stopped throwing pebbles at her and instead noticed just how lovely she was.

Adina tilted her chin to the side, gazing adoringly up at Tikva. "I think you are beautiful too."

A flush warmed Tikva's cheeks. She was tempted to argue, since the last time she'd studied her own reflection in a pool of still water after a heavy rain, the wan visage and drawn features had nearly made her weep. She'd been aware of her natural beauty as a child, something she'd been complimented on many times over the years, but it, like her youth and health, had been siphoned away—one more punishment from Adonai, no doubt, for her pride and vanity. But instead of contradicting Adina's sweet words, Tikva pressed a silent kiss to her forehead.

"I don't remember her," Adina said with a sigh.

"I know, sweet girl. I wish I could tell you more. Ask your abba."

"He has told me a few things, but it makes him sad to speak of her, and I do not like to see him sad."

Tikva had rarely seen Simcha without a smile on his face, unless he was fussing over her or ordering her to rest. It hurt her own heart to hear that grief still clung to the man who'd been so good to her all these years.

"I wish *you* were my mother. My abba would be a good husband to you. And he is lonely, I can tell." The plea in Adina's eyes made Tikva's heart squeeze painfully.

After the discussion about living arrangements a few weeks ago she'd hoped Adina might allow the idea to drop, but apparently it had only burgeoned into something far too complicated to explain to an innocent child. Simcha was a good man, and perhaps someday another woman would see the generous spirit and innate kindness that resided at his core and take Rachel's place, but it could not be Tikva. "I will not marry again," she said.

"Why not?" Adina pressed. "Do you not like my abba?"

"Of course I do. Your abba is a wonderful man," Tikva said. "He is the best of fathers, and I have no doubt that he was a husband of great honor to your imma."

"Then why not be married to him? You could be my imma. You wouldn't have to walk back and forth every day. I would cook for you," she said, her tone becoming a plea. "My abba says you need to eat more before your bones waste away." Tears formed in her eyes, and she threw her arms around Tikva, her face pressed into Tikva's neck as a sob burst free. "Please, don't leave me."

◆

Before Adina's cheeks had even dried, and well before Tikva was able to assuage her fears, a group of four girls close to her age appeared at the edge of the stream.

Wiping her face clear of the evidence of her tears, Adina watched as the four bounded into the water, wordless and wide-eyed as they splashed and giggled fifteen paces away.

Tikva, too, watched the group of girls with a growing realization that she'd very rarely seen Adina in the presence of other children. Whenever she'd asked whether the girl would like to go outside and play with friends, Adina had shrugged off the suggestion, insisting that she much more enjoyed working alongside Tikva with the clay, making meals, or even aiding Helena in the market. But it was evident now by the expression of longing on her face that none of that had been true. Adina was desperate for friends her own age.

"Do you know those girls?" Tikva asked.

Adina shook her head.

"Why don't you introduce yourself? They seem to be having fun."

Adina shifted her feet in the water. "I'd rather not."

"Why?"

With a sigh, she shrugged her narrow shoulders, making Tikva consider just what sort of weight they carried. "I do not fit in with other children," she said.

"What does that mean?" Tikva asked.

Adina did not answer but continued watching the girls, even as a bevy of memories from Tikva's own girlhood pressed upward. On many days just like this one, when the sun was relentless and even the usual ocean breeze missing, she and her cousins Lilah and Margalit had raced to the banks of this very same stream, plunging into the cool water and chattering like sparrows as they joked and laughed together. Many were the secrets shared between the three as they grew up together. In fact, it was not far from this very spot that Tikva shared the news with Lilah and Margalit that she would soon marry Asa. And yet neither of her cousins had spoken to her since it had become common knowledge in Ptolemais that Tikva was perpetually unclean. The friendships she'd once considered unbreakable had been yet another casualty to this horrific affliction.

Heart aching, both from the memories and for her young friend, Tikva placed a palm beneath Adina's chin. "You are the kindest girl I know, Adina, full of bright enthusiasm and keen intelligence. If anyone gets the chance to know you they will be just as glad for your friendship as I am."

Tears swam in Adina's eyes. "Sometimes the other children make fun of my abba," she said. "Of the way he walks and uses his hands."

Frustration and guilt swept through Tikva. She'd been so wrapped up in her own hurts, she'd not realized that Adina, too, suffered from rejection by others in the town.

"The only thing you can do is try," said Tikva, swallowing the lump that formed in her throat. "Just reach out and see what happens. You cannot know how they will receive you if you do not make an attempt."

After a few more moments of gazing at the circle of girls, with desperation for connection plain on her precious face, Adina nodded. "All right, I will try."

As Tikva watched Simcha's brave daughter square her shoulders and push through the shallow stream toward the girls, her own chest pulsed with nervous anticipation.

When two of the girls swung around to greet her, asking her name and inviting her to join them, Tikva nearly cheered aloud at how Adina's steps of faith had been rewarded.

Tikva retreated to the edge of the stream, seating herself in the dappled shade of a yew tree, prepared to wait for as long as Adina needed with her new friends. Simcha would understand the delay. Leaning her head against the trunk of the tree, she breathed deeply, thinking over Helena's entreaty that she consider going to this Greek physician in Caesarea.

Over the past few days, Helena had not allowed the subject to pass away. When she was not regaling Tikva with tales of those who'd been treated by the man named Damianos and the positive changes wrought by his treatments, she was telling stories of people she'd known back in Thessalonica and the supposed cures some of them had experienced at similar centers of healing. The thought of enduring any more treatments, no matter how promising, made Tikva's stomach churn in dread. And yet, watching Adina with her new friends, laughing and carefree, Tikva could not help but wonder what life might be like if she were finally free of this burden. If she were clean and whole, she'd be able to forge new friendships or possibly rebuild those she'd lost. She'd be able to attend the synagogue, wash her body in a *mikveh*, even perhaps set foot inside the Court of Women at the Temple in Jerusalem. And maybe, if he had not changed his mind, she could reconsider Simcha's proposal of marriage. The thought of joining herself with such a kind and honorable man, one whose daughter she adored, was more than she could dream of.

She shook her head with a huff of laughter at herself. Even if she did give in to Helena's persuasion, and even if by some fantastic miracle the Greek physician could help, Simcha would not be interested in marriage to her. Since the day he'd proposed a union and she'd turned him down, he'd not said another word about it. No—there was no reason to indulge in pointless imaginings about such things.

Two women approached the stream, one raising a hand and calling out to Adina's new friends. When they reached the edge of the water, they conversed for a few moments with the girls, Adina included.

Adina turned back to point in Tikva's direction, and the gaze of the two women followed her gesture.

Even from where she sat, some thirty paces away, Tikva could see the backs of both women stiffen. They glanced between them and then waved to the girls to leave the stream. As if time had slowed to a crawl, Tikva watched in horror as the girls darted out of the stream, leaving Adina alone in the very center. Without turning back to offer farewells, they followed the two women back toward the city.

Adina's shoulders bowed, her chin dropping nearly to her chest. Tikva surged to her feet, ignoring the increasingly familiar fatigue that had settled into her bones as she sat beneath the tree and fought against her thundering pulse. By the time she reached Adina and pulled the girl around to face her, her hands were shaking.

"What happened?" Tikva asked, dreading the answer.

Adina pressed her lips together, her eyes darting away. "They had to go home with their mothers."

"Did they say something to you?"

Adina shook her head, dark curls gleaming in the sunlight, but sadness brewed within the depths of the rich brown eyes she'd inherited from her abba.

"Adina. Tell me what those women said to you," Tikva pressed, unrepentant at her commanding tone. She'd never had to raise her voice to Adina, who was the most compliant child she'd ever met, but she could not bear the pain in her expression.

She drew in a wobbly breath, still not meeting Tikva's gaze. "At first they were kind. They greeted me and asked my name. But when they asked where my mother was..." She sighed again, her voice trailing into a whisper. "I told them I was here with you instead."

That must have been the moment both women had turned to look at Tikva, undoubtedly recognizing the Unclean Woman of Ptolemais.

Adina's voice was impossibly small as she continued. "What does *zavah* mean? They said their children could not be with me, that I was tainted." Her eyes glistened. "They said I was just as unclean as you."

Being forced to explain purity laws, especially to a girl who'd not yet begun her own monthly cycles, was disconcerting, but from the curiosity in Adina's expression, Tikva considered that doing so would spare Simcha the task.

Therefore, Tikva told Adina of what would soon happen to her body and how a woman was considered unclean until her flow ceased for seven days, when she could wash in the mikveh and be pure once again.

Adina's brow furrowed in confusion. "Then, once you are clean again, will they allow me to come near their daughters?"

Tikva's throat burned with unshed tears. "No, my sweet girl. My body refuses to stop bleeding. So instead of being called *niddah,* which is the monthly condition, I am perpetually in a state of zavah. It has not ceased for the length of your lifetime. I will always be unclean. I will never be able to dip in the mikveh and become pure." *And therefore, I will always taint those around me with my presence.*

"Is that why you are sick?" Adina asked.

Tikva nodded, her throat now too tight to speak.

Adina tilted her chin, looking up at Tikva with a sincere expression that reminded her very much of Simcha. "Then I have no need of them." She flung her hand in the direction the girls had fled with their sour-faced mothers. "I have all the friends I need." And for the second time that day, she flung her arms about Tikva and hugged her fiercely, reminding her that she was only one of two people—Helena being the other—who touched Tikva without reservation.

And as the two of them stood in the stream, cool water flowing about their ankles toward the sea, Tikva changed her mind. It did not matter that the thought of submitting to yet another embarrassing examination by yet another physician was abhorrent or that she had no idea what sort of stomach-churning treatment she might have to endure. She'd do anything for this child. Anything.

CHAPTER NINE

❖

"Your mother-in-law cannot come inside," said the young woman, compassion in her kohl-lined eyes. "Only those who seek healing are to enter. And you will be here until tomorrow, so I would advise that she find a place to pass the night."

Tikva turned to Helena, fear and doubt taking up equal portions of her heart as she gripped her mother-in-law's arm. "The entire night?"

Helena patted Tikva's hand. "It will be all right, my dear. I have a friend here in Caesarea. I have no doubt she and her family will give me shelter until the morning. I will be back to meet you here then." She brushed her lips across Tikva's cheek. "Go now. The sooner the physician meets with you, the sooner you will be healed."

The unshakable faith Tikva's mother-in-law had in this Greek physician was something she'd not yet been able to embrace. Since the day Tikva had agreed to go to Caesarea, for Adina's sake, Helena had been adamant that not only was she making a wise choice but that she should consider whether it was Adonai who'd provided this path to Tikva's healing.

Just imagine, Helena had said, her eyes brimming with tears of gratitude, *a world-renowned Greek physician, coming to Israel just at the time you needed him. It is a miracle in and of itself!*

In fact, she was so full of joy after Tikva had given in that she did not bother to question why, if Adonai's hand was in this solution, he had not brought the Greek to her twelve years ago. As for Tikva, she felt no rush of hope from the decision, nor any assurance that this might finally be the answer. But for Adina's sake, and for Helena's, Tikva vowed to endure.

So she said nothing as Helena bartered with a local fisherman for passage on his boat to the port at Caesarea this morning, nor as they'd cut through the blue, blue water of the Great Sea. Nothing as they walked through the bustling city where Herod's grand, shining palace perched above the seashore. Nothing as they stood in front of the large dwelling wherein the Greek physician had set up his house of healing. And nothing as Helena explained Tikva's situation and then handed over the remainder of her dowry to the young woman at the door.

But as soon as the door closed behind Tikva's back, panic wound its way around her throat, and the immediate instinct to run seized her. Noticing her hesitation, the young woman looped her arm through Tikva's and offered a gentle smile.

"Come," she said, guiding her around the large water clock in the main foyer and into the hallway. "There is no need to fear. Damianos will be able to help you, I have no doubt."

Although Tikva still had the urge to pull away from the woman, the farther down the hall they walked the more curiosity drove her onward. Gentle lyre music floated through the air from somewhere in the house, a lovely tune that reminded her of flowing water, one that softened the sharpest edges of her panic as they moved deeper into the household.

The young woman led Tikva to a small chamber, at the center of which stood a thick cedar pedestal that stood almost hip high and that was covered in a long red cushion three fingers thick.

"Please," said the woman, gesturing to the bed. "Lie down and relax. Damianos has a few others to tend to this afternoon, but he will join you soon."

"You are leaving?" Tikva asked, unnerved by the thought that she'd be forced to wait and wishing again that Helena had been allowed to stay.

"I won't be far," said the young woman, turning to light an oil lamp on a nearby table, as well as a small incense burner. "Call out if you have need of me."

"I do not know your name," Tikva said as she pulled herself atop the downy cushion and laid her head on the softest pillow she'd ever felt. Whatever herbs the woman had placed in the burner began to emit an odor Tikva had never smelled before, something that reminded her of fertile soil and flowers in full bloom.

The woman pulled a fine wool blanket over Tikva's body, tucking it beneath her arms and legs. "I am Agathe, Damianos's wife. Now rest," she said, brushing Tikva's hair away from her face with a soft, rhythmic touch. "Take long, deep breaths and do not worry anymore."

After Agathe exited the room, leaving the door cracked open a handspan, a wave of weariness came over Tikva, as if her mind had finally caught up to her body.

However nervous Tikva had been to be separated from Helena, Agathe did seem to be kind. And although her mother-in-law had been forthcoming about her circumstances, the young woman had not hesitated to touch her. Like the day Adina had hugged her so fiercely in the stream, she realized how wonderful it was to be treated as if she were normal. As if she were clean.

Her doubts began to wither away as she sank farther into the softness of the pillow and the cushion that protected her boney spine from pressing against the bed stand.

The music from the other room wafted through the open door, the lyre being joined by a flute and a hand drum. It had been so long since Tikva had been given the luxury of rest and years since she'd enjoyed the slide of soft fabrics against her skin. Her eyelids grew heavy, and she allowed the sweet music to lull her to sleep until a soft voice roused her by speaking her name. When she opened her eyes, a man with gray at his temples looked down on her, a sympathetic expression on his lightly wrinkled face.

"Hello," he said. "I am Damianos. Agathe has explained your troubles to me, but I must examine you to further understand how I can be of help to you."

Tikva had endured many such examinations, most by midwives, but a few that left her in tears. Her heart began to thrum as she clutched the blanket tighter to her chest.

"Do not be frightened," said Damianos. "Agathe is here." He gestured to his wife standing nearby. "You are safe."

His gentle words did little to assuage her fears, but for Adina's sake, she nodded, latched her eyes on the ceiling above her, and braced for the intrusion. Hopefully, the last she would ever suffer.

❖

It did not matter that Damianos had been gentle, nor that he'd murmured assurances throughout the examination, and Agathe had held her hand. Tikva's jaw hurt from gritting her teeth for the entire time. That anyone had intimate knowledge of her condition was embarrassing enough, but that a strange man's hands had poked and prodded at her uncovered body left her blazing with humiliation.

Once he'd finally allowed Agathe to replace the blanket, Damianos pressed his fingers into the skin of her arm, stuck them into her mouth to look at her teeth and tongue, peered into her eyes with close scrutiny, and then clapped his hands together with a satisfied grunt.

"I can help you, without a doubt," he said. "You will begin to see changes by tomorrow."

Tikva gaped at the physician. After all this time? After all the men who'd told her it was hopeless? After all the midwives who'd declared her incurable? How could this man dare state such a thing with confidence?

"What is to be done?" she asked. "I have been bleeding for twelve years, my lord."

He grinned. "You must trust me, dear. I have seen many things in the House of Asclepius, things that would astound you."

"Asclepius?" Tikva repeated.

"Don't you know that is where you are?" He gestured to the painting behind her head. She twisted her neck to find a brightly painted mural of a man holding a staff, upon which curled an enormous reptile. "It is to him that our people offer service and from him which healing originates."

A deep shiver began at her very core. In stark contrast to his seemingly benign words, her mind reacted violently to the idea that it was no simple home she'd entered.

"This is a temple?" she asked, attempting to keep her voice from warbling.

"Of sorts," said Damianos. "I have come to Caesarea to begin practicing here, and since there is no dedicated sanctuary built as yet, those in need of my services are welcomed into my home."

An image of her father's face rose in her mind, as did the words he'd spoken day after day about the One True God and the jealousy Adonai had for His people. Her entire body stiffened, and her gaze darted to the doorway. Could she reach the exit before Agathe and Damianos grabbed ahold of her?

Damianos must have seen the panic on her face, for his hands came down on her shoulders. "Breathe slowly, Tikva. There is no need to be frightened. I know exactly what is wrong with your body and why you have been expelling blood for so long."

Even as confused and uneasy as she was, his calm statement snagged her interest.

"Tell me," she said.

"There are four humors," he said. "Blood, phlegm, yellow bile, and black bile. When these are out of balance, your body will strive to reassert its natural state. In your case, somehow the interrupted pregnancy threw your body out of balance. You simply have too much blood, my dear."

Tikva considered this information, her mind reeling from ideas she'd never heard before. He sounded so confident in his assessment, so self-assured in his knowledge, far more than anyone Helena had brought to her after she miscarried, to be sure. Perhaps she'd been too hasty in pushing aside his help at the mention of a foreign god.

And truly, what had Adonai done? She'd prayed for years for a solution. She'd repented over and over of any sin she might have committed in ignorance. She'd washed her body in water retrieved from the sacred pool of Siloam in Jerusalem, where the faithful dipped in the enormous mikveh before going up to the Temple. She'd even drunk water from that same spring-fed pool after Helena had heard of miraculous healings there. Tikva had no doubt that Adonai was the Creator of all, and she had no interest in worshipping this Asclepius, but surely a man who knew so much, who studied all over the world and treated people far more important than she, must understand the workings of the body, no matter which gods he served.

"I am Hebrew," she said. "I worship Adonai alone."

He brushed her concerns aside with a swipe of his palm. "It matters not. I can still help."

Torn between the uncertainty in her own soul and the confidence in this physician's steady gaze, she closed her eyes, reminding herself why she was here in the first place. She'd vowed to try. Vowed that Adina's needs came before her own, and if she walked away from this place the sacrifice of the last of her dowry would be for nothing. Hadn't her father turned away? Perhaps Adonai had done the same.

With a long sigh, she relaxed her body, uncurled her white-knuckled fingers from the blanket, and agreed to undergo whatever treatment was necessary to restore the balance of her humors, whatever that might mean.

Agathe patted her hands with a wide, reassuring smile. Then she fetched a small vial of herb-scented oil and anointed Tikva's head while Damianos went to fetch the tools he said were required to treat her.

Agathe moved the incense burner across the room, bringing it close to Tikva's head, and placed another handful of something inside the smoldering bowl. Again that rich, earthy-floral scent invaded the room and, after a few deep breaths, the tension in her body began to uncoil.

Damianos returned, carrying an ivory inlaid box. He laid it on the bed near her feet, his lips moving silently as he pressed his palms to the lid, head bowed.

As the physician dipped his hands in a bowl of what to Tikva's nose smelled of watered-down wine, Agathe brought her a cup of hot tea, something that might be bitter if it were not for the generous measure of honey she'd added. She told Tikva that it would be best for her stomach to remain empty for now but that in the morning she would be provided with a sumptuous meal to break her fast.

Then Damianos opened the box and lifted a long instrument, one that even to a now-drowsy Tikva looked to be razor-sharp.

"What will you do?" she mumbled through heavy lips. "Not... Not inside..."

"No, my dear," said Damianos, smoothing a cold palm down the length of her arm before grasping her elbow tightly. "Only your arms. And perhaps your legs if the flow is not enough."

Her eyelids flickered, her mind soggy with confusion and her limbs beginning to numb. Then, just as Damianos drew the instrument across the skin of her upper arm, a sharp pain jolted through her. She tried to shy away from the hurt and felt Agathe's hands pressing her down to the bed with surprising force. With a plea that never made it to her lips, she fought a swirling wave of heaviness. The fleeting thought of whether this was what it had felt like for Asa as he drowned swam through her mind. Then, when another sting of agony cut into her other arm, blackness won the fight.

◆

When she awoke, the room was nearly dark, just the one oil lamp still guttering on the table. Although the incense was no longer burning, the heavy floral scent still filled the room. The chamber was small, perhaps five paces across and eight long, with three narrow slits near the ceiling to let in air and light. Tikva could see the glint of two stars through the gaps.

Agathe and Damianos were no longer there, but it did not take long for Tikva to remember the bloodletting they'd subjected her to. Her arms and legs ached and, glancing down, she saw that they'd been wrapped in linen, but her head was so light she was forced to lay it back down on the pillow.

The music was still wending its way into the room, but the tone of it had changed. No longer gentle and soothing, the stringed instruments now plucked out a haunting tune that more closely resembled the dark, churning sea than the gently flowing stream from before. A chill brushed up her spine, the chamber having cooled while she slept.

She wondered what else she'd slept through. Had Damianos done more to her than draw blood from her broken body? Should she call out for Agathe and demand answers? Demand to leave this place? If only Helena had come with her, she'd know what to do. Tears gathered in her eyes, then dripped down her cheeks. She never should have submitted to any of this. How could cutting open the skin of her arms and legs lessen the flow from her womb? She'd been a fool to not flee at the first niggle of doubt. Thanks be to Adonai that her father could not see her now, lying in a house of pagan worship, having turned her back on everything she knew out of desperation.

A tortured cry began in some far reach of the house, the wail making Tikva bolt upright on the bed, chest heaving and spikes of pain shooting down her limbs from the swift movement. Both the sound and the pain were forgotten, however, when she caught a glimpse of a long shadow sliding over the threshold.

Narrowing her eyes, she held her breath as she peered at the shadow, which stretched and undulated over the floor, clinging to the wall as it slithered along. Every hair on Tikva's neck rose to attention. There was a serpent in this room. One that looked to be nearly twice as long as Tikva's body.

She'd never been frightened of snakes, having come across many in the past few years on her daily treks between her home, Simcha's, and the market. But paired with the strange music, the deep shadows, the terrifying treatment she'd endured, and the eerie cries, sharing this small chamber with such a terrifying creature was more than Tikva could bear. She opened her mouth and drowned out the plaintive cry with a scream of her own before the darkness consumed her again and she knew no more.

CHAPTER TEN

◆

Her eyes opened slowly, the ceiling above blurring as sunlight flooded through the window. Although the dream that still clung like a poison vine told Tikva she was still in the Greek physician's house, it was the familiar crumbling plaster overhead that reminded her she was in her own bed at home.

The past two days were a haze. She remembered waking to Agathe standing above her, that same placid smile contrasting the horrors Tikva had endured the night before. She also remembered asking the physician's wife about the serpent and was told that she'd been blessed by a vision of Asclepius himself and that the dream meant she would indeed be healed. An explanation that Tikva did not believe at all, since she'd been wide awake when that serpent entered her room.

But after she'd been given a mug of fish broth that tasted strongly of the sea, along with a handful of olives and a bowl of barley mash—nothing like the sumptuous meal she'd been promised—and ushered out the door to meet Helena on the front steps, the rest of the journey home had been nothing more than a fog of pain and exhaustion.

Blinking her eyes, she rolled to her side, finding linen bandages still wrapped around her upper arms and thighs. She winced at the sight, remembering the slice of the blade against her skin and the sensation of Agathe holding her down as Damianos cut her. It was a miracle she'd lived to see the next day.

"Oh!" came Helena's voice from across the room. "You are awake!"

Her mother-in-law bustled across the space, gesturing for her to lie back down. "You are not strong enough to arise, daughter. Rest. I will bring you something to eat."

"I must...take care of my needs," Tikva said.

"Oh my. Of course," said Helena, then offered her hands to Tikva in assistance. The burn of the wounds against the raspy bandages nearly brought tears to Tikva's eyes, but somehow between the two of them, she managed to stand.

Helena turned to meal preparation as Tikva began her morning ablutions. But when the time came to replace her rags, they were not soiled at all. Not one spot of red marred the fabric in her hand.

Bewildered, Tikva nearly called out for Helena but stopped herself. The hideous experience at the home of the physician was still fresh in her mind, as were the serious misgivings she had about his claims after putting her through such torture.

Helena had been so hopeful as they'd traveled to Caesarea, expounding on the many wonders of her homeland and the brilliance of its people, and so thrilled when the physician allowed Tikva entrance to his house of healing that Tikva hesitated to give credence to anything Damianos had done.

Surely, this must be a coincidence. There had been many days in the last twelve years when her body did not bleed, but never more than two or three in a row, and never enough to be declared ritually clean.

Unless it was actually proven that something had indeed changed within her, she would not raise Helena's hopes, or her own. And if that seventh day came, and she doubted it would, only then would she consider whether the physician's claims were actually worth believing. Until then, she'd go about as she always did, pressing onward, until Adonai deemed her time on earth complete. She prayed that her entrance into the temple of a foreign god did not hasten her end further.

◈

Three days the rags had gone without stain. Three days she'd held in the nervous anticipation and the tentative hope that fought its way to the surface each morning she opened her eyes.

Had something truly altered within the depths of her body? She felt no change. She was just as fatigued as ever, the familiar aches still constant as she pushed the cart back and forth between Simcha's house and the market. But perhaps if the bleeding had stopped, so too would the effects of its loss. She'd still not said anything to Helena, but if her rags remained unsullied for at least another few days, she knew she would not be able to keep it to herself.

She paused in the journey to wipe her brow, wincing at the tenderness from the wound Damianos inflicted in her arm, and was surprised to find Adina skipping toward her like she had when she was small. It was rare that Simcha allowed his daughter to meet her on the road, but the delighted smile on the girl's face and her pleasure that Tikva had returned made Tikva grateful that she had. It gave her the boost to her spirits that she needed to finish the trek back to Simcha's home.

After she'd delivered the empty cart to the side of the house and submitted to Adina's insistence that she partake of a small meal and drink some water, Tikva left the girl to sweep a few cobwebs from the corners with a long-handled broom and went out to the workshop to deliver a message from Helena.

Seated at his potter's wheel, a strange contraption built so he could spin the round stone with his feet, Simcha positioned his hands around the lip of the jar he was forming, his expert fingers smoothing and molding the clay as it turned around and around.

The process had always been fascinating to Tikva, and watching Simcha, who was nothing less than a master, was enthralling. The limitations of his crooked leg and the malformations of his fingers had no bearing on his skill. Each item was fashioned with care, whether it was a cooking pot or an ornamental vase. Simcha threw his entire being into every piece, something that was evident from the intense furrow of his brow whenever he worked the clay and how he barely acknowledged anything around him when he was deep in his craft.

Grateful for the opportunity to observe him without notice, Tikva took advantage of his concentration and watched Simcha form a bland cylinder into a fluted vase with a spindly neck that seemed almost too delicate to hold its head aloft.

Once the rotation of the wheel ceased and Simcha raised his own head, the spell was broken. He craned his neck to one side and then the other, stretching the tension that must surely reside there after such intensive activity.

"It's beautiful," said Tikva, approaching the wheel to examine the vase.

Simcha's smile was the mirror image of his daughter's, something that she'd noticed, of course, but today when little sprouts of hope had been forcing their way upward, the sight made something flit about in her stomach. Something she'd not felt in years…since Asa.

Clearing her throat of the surprise such a thought inspired, she continued. "Helena asked me to tell you that she had three customers request double-wicked oil lamps like the one you created last week. It seems to be a popular item, so she wonders if you might make a few more."

"Certainly," he said. "When I am finished with this piece and the incense burner commissioned by that centurion, I'll work on that."

Simcha could not compete with the large pottery workshops where many hands churned out piece after piece, nor the ships that carried exotic foreign-made goods, but the quality of craftsmanship and Helena's superior bargaining skills ensured that they sold just enough to keep the four of them fed. Any special commission was a welcome one indeed.

And of course without her dowry to fall back on now, they must make every effort to sell as many pieces as possible. But perhaps, if Tikva's body was truly healed, she would be able to work harder, move faster, and maybe even learn the wheel herself in order to help Simcha grow the business beyond its current limits.

"How does it spin so quickly?" she asked, curiosity bubbling out of her in a way it hadn't in some time.

Surprise widened Simcha's eyes as he took in her question. In all the years that Tikva had come into this workshop, treaded clay, and delivered his creations, she'd never shown outward interest in the actual process. A swell of guilt came over her as she realized she'd been far too absorbed in her own concerns to even ask about how he'd become such a proficient potter.

"Would you like to try?" he asked, a gleam of excitement coming into his brown eyes.

A week ago, she would not have bothered to attempt such a thing, knowing that bending her body into such a position might well cause her more pain than it was worth, especially with the gashes that were only now beginning to scab over on her arms and legs. But today, after three days of clean rags, she'd push aside the discomfort and take the chance. She nodded.

After he'd carefully removed the finished vase from the working platform and moved it onto a nearby shelf to dry, he gestured for Tikva to sit astride the wooden seat and place a foot on the flywheel below. Feeling a little foolish in such a precarious position, with her tunic tucked around her legs, she suppressed a laugh behind her palm.

"I feel as though I might topple over," she said, adjusting her hips to stabilize herself and pressing her bare foot against the stone to watch the surface begin a slow rotation. "How do you sit here for hours?"

"I'm used to it after so many years," he said. "It is no different from breathing now. The wheel has become another part of me, like an additional limb."

She smiled at the comparison. "Well, I'm afraid I might break your 'limb,' my friend."

He laughed. "You won't. It is very sturdy. My own father built it before I was born. It has lasted this long, I am certain it can survive your slight weight." He hobbled across the workshop to scoop a bit of raw clay from a covered pot and then slapped the lump atop the smooth surface.

"I can't do what you do," Tikva protested, palms in the air.

"Perhaps not," he said, a hint of mischief curving his lips. "But I am a very good teacher."

Caught up in his enthusiasm, Tikva agreed to try and spent the next few minutes turning the flywheel with her foot as Simcha demonstrated how to shape the formless lump into some semblance of a bowl. When she finally consented to trying with her own hands, she was shocked when he squashed down the clay, dashed some water over it, and made her start from the beginning.

Simcha showed her how to press her thumbs into the center and how to draw up the clay into a cylinder that would then be stretched outward to form the distinct shape. He was nothing but patient, encouraging her at every step, and pressing her to not give up when one portion of the rim caved in.

More tender shoots of hope burst through the rocky soil, defying the effort she normally exerted against the effects Simcha's kindness had on her thirsty soul. But even more than his calm voice in her ear and the bright notes of his laughter, it was the few times he brushed his fingers over hers as he guided her in the process that truly made her heart take flight. It was the first time the two of them had ever come into physical contact in the many years she'd known him, but not once did he flinch or shy away from her touch.

By the time the wheel stopped spinning, her body was aching for a reprieve and her wounds were throbbing, but it had indeed been worth the pain. Her attempt at a bowl was uneven and marred by lumps and gouges, but she was thrilled by her creation.

"It is perfect!" said Simcha.

Tikva laughed at his false declaration. "It is nothing of the sort." She turned the wheel with her hand to examine the far side, where the rim looked more like a wave than one of Simcha's smooth edges.

"For a first try, it is nothing short of magnificent," he insisted as he slid a thin cord beneath the bowl to release it from the surface. "We shall allow it to dry, and then I'll teach you how to fire it as well."

She looked up at the man who'd offered her so much in the years since her life crumbled in on her—a means of survival, distraction from her daily burden, the chance to know his daughter, and most of all, unhindered friendship—and the flicker that had begun with his smile sparked into a tentative but promising flame.

Perhaps these three days were a new beginning, a start to something she'd dared not even pray for.

◆

No longer was she able to contain the gasp of relief this morning as she inspected her rags. Never had her broken body gone six days without an issue of blood since her tiny babe was taken from her womb.

Helena darted across the room, hands coated in half-mixed bread dough. "What is it? Tikva? Did one of the wounds begin to bleed again?"

Tikva turned to face her mother-in-law, tears fogging her sight. "I did not want to say anything yet. You were so hopeful...."

Helena's eyes widened. "Tell me what?"

"I thought perhaps it was a coincidence," Tikva said. "After that horrible night with the Greek—"

Helena lifted one doughy palm to cover her mouth. "I wish I'd never sent you there. Oh my daughter, please forgive me. I'll never forget the sight of you leaving that place, so pale. Dazed and blood soaking your bandages... If that basket weaver had not been walking by and willing to help us to the boat, I don't know how I would even have gotten you home. I was so wrong to ask you to go. And now all your money is gone—"

Tikva lifted the rag in front of her. "No. Helena, look. It's clean. They've been clean for six mornings in a row."

Bewildered, her mother-in-law's face twisted as she gazed at the unsullied linen. "I don't understand."

"Yes, that place was horrible. They cut me and frightened me out of my wits. But somehow, someway, I think they might have healed me."

Helena released a startled gasp. "Do you think so?"

"Only time can tell us. It has been six days, and I could not even attempt to be declared clean until the seventh. I would guess it might even take me a while to prove that I am no longer zavah. But perhaps…" She shrugged. "Perhaps you were right, and Adonai provided a way. Not the way I could have guessed, nor the way I would have chosen. But who is to know the mind of the Creator?"

"Oh my daughter. I do hope it is so. I knew the stories I'd heard of the healers from Greece could not have all been falsehoods. There had to have been some truth in them." She shook her head as if marveling at such a thing. "And just think, if you are healed, you can begin joining me in the marketplace and help me sell Simcha's pottery. Perhaps you might even reconsider the offer he gave you?"

A flush built in Tikva's cheeks, as the same thought had occurred to her far too many times over the past week, especially after their time together over the pottery wheel.

But she brushed the idea away again, as she'd done every time it pressed its way upward. There was no use cradling such lovely thoughts to her breast until she knew for sure.

"We won't know until tomorrow," said Tikva. "And I cannot consider anything else until then. I feel little different than I did before I went to Caesarea, except perhaps a little less soreness inside my mouth. But this could all be false hope."

"True," said her mother-in-law, her eyes glimmering. "But it could also be something wonderful."

◆

In a haze Tikva stared at the red rag on the seventh morning, every traitorous hope she'd stupidly allowed herself over the past week dissolving into cold reality. Blinking her eyes of the futile tears, she shook off Helena's soothing grip on her shoulders and walked out the door. This was her life, such as it was, and it was all it would ever be. She had a job to do.

CHAPTER ELEVEN

◆

Two months later

The cart wobbled and tipped to the side. With all the strength she had left in her, Tikva managed to keep it from toppling completely when the wheel juddered and separated itself from the axle, rolling into the weeds. As the cart jolted to a heavy, tilted stop, the load of Simcha's work she'd been transporting to the market shivered and clattered, making Tikva gasp in dismay as she heard the distinct sound of pottery shattering.

Once she was assured that the cart was secure, if not fully upright, Tikva moved to inspect the damage. Two of Simcha's newly designed double-wick lamps were in pieces, and one jug was missing its handle, but the destruction was not nearly as terrible as it could have been. But even more worrisome was the broken wheel, which was lying a few paces away in the weeds at the side of the road.

Tikva brushed her palms down her face with a groan. How would she move on with the pottery if she could not even lift the heavy wooden wheel? She certainly had no means to repair it.

Looking south back toward Simcha's house, she noted that the road was still deserted, early as it was. Tikva usually enjoyed making these journeys just after dawn, when there was no one on the road to sneer at her or make comments that the proper place for a woman in the state of zavah was in seclusion. Did they truly believe she should have been sequestered in her home for the past twelve years?

Looking north, toward the city, she determined that way too was barren. She might have to wait an hour or two for anyone to come by, and there was no guarantee that when someone did appear, they would even bother to help.

She wondered whether Simcha might worry about her and come after a while, but there had been many days she'd not returned from the market directly after her second trip to deliver pots, choosing instead to go to her spot on the bluff above the sea and stare out at the water and torture herself with dreams of what might have been, had Asa's boat appeared on that horizon that day.

She could not leave the cart full of Simcha's valuable creations on the side of the road, so there was nothing to do now but wait.

A short while after she'd settled herself down in the weeds, her assumptions were proven correct. Although a number of townspeople walked by her, most took no more than a second glance before hurrying on by. She was the famous Unclean Woman of Ptolemais, and no matter how she tried to hide her face behind veils, her gaunt figure and occupation pushing the pottery cart was well known.

As the sun lifted higher into the sky, she allowed her thoughts to wander as she watched the wispy clouds meander along. It had been nearly two months since the blood had returned and she'd been forced to accept, once and for all, that there was no miracle for her. Since that day she'd let go of the foolish idea of being a mother to Adina, or a wife to Simcha, and embraced the limited role she had in both their lives.

She'd not entertained Simcha's urgings to learn more of the pottery wheel, nor did she venture any farther than his home with Adina. She'd been thoughtless to be seen with the girl at the stream and did not want to further damage Adina's chances of making friends. She may not be in full seclusion like she had been in the beginning of this affliction, but her world now consisted almost entirely of the home she shared with Helena and the road between Ptolemais and Simcha's house. That was her lot, and she would be content with it.

The awful morning when Tikva had discovered that her rags were stained again, Helena had tried to apologize for her terrible judgment in convincing her to go to Caesarea, but Tikva had refused to even allow her to finish the thought. "What's done is done," she'd said. "It was my choice to go." And then she'd informed Helena that any talk of physicians, healers, and miracles were not to be discussed in their home again. It was the most unyielding she'd ever been with the woman who'd saved her life in so many ways, but it was necessary.

Thankfully, her mother-in-law had respected her wishes and let the matter fade into nothing, even if the scars on her arms and legs would never disappear. And today, as she waited for Simcha to rescue her, it was the furthest thing from her mind. Instead, she basked in the warmth of the sunshine on her upturned face, breathing in the sea salt air with her eyes closed.

"Shalom, young woman, can we be of help?" came a voice from nearby. Tikva's eyelids flew open to find four beggars, two women and two men, standing a few paces away.

The older woman who'd spoken came closer, her gaze on Tikva as the two men moved to peer into the cart. Did they mean to rob her? Here in the middle of the day?

Heart pounding, her gaze flitted back and forth between the dirty, threadbare beggars and the empty road, knowing that even if her cries were heard it was doubtful that anyone would come to her aid.

"Please, don't take anything. They aren't mine," pleaded Tikva, her voice warbling at the thought that all Simcha's hard work, pieces that took him hours upon hours to create, might be whisked away by thieves.

Raising her palms in a show of peace, the beggar-woman took another hesitant step forward. "We mean you no harm, my lady. And we certainly have no need for your wares on our travels. But my man there might be able to fix your wheel, if you'd like." She jerked her chin to the tallest of the males, whose clothes looked to have been scavenged from a rag pile and whose grin was missing more teeth than it possessed.

"Easy," he lisped as he limped into the weeds to fetch the wheel. "Have you back on the road in no time at all."

Speechless, Tikva stared at the men as they carried the wooden wheel between them and then set about repairing the cart. Within only a few minutes, they'd retrieved the axle pin, which had dislodged itself and fallen into the road, and her rickety vehicle was restored to working order.

"There now," said the first woman with a satisfied clap of her filthy hands. "All done."

Unbidden, tears misted Tikva's eyes and relief flooded her chest. "I can't...thank you," she said, unsure of how to talk to people such as these. She had compassion for them, of course, but aside from the few encounters she'd had in the marketplace, whenever one of them approached her to plead for a mite or two, she'd never had a conversation with a beggar.

"You are certainly welcome," said the woman with a tight smile that made it clear she'd discerned Tikva's thoughts with ease. Then she turned to her companions with a wave of her arms. "Come, friends, we have far to travel."

Just as the group moved to obey her command, Tikva's spirit prickled with shame. Here she'd immediately thought these people meant to steal from her and made no attempt to hide her suspicion, when they were the only people that had bothered to stop and help her.

"Please!" she said as she scrambled to her feet. "Forgive my rudeness. Thank you for your kindness. You did not have to stop."

The woman's brows furrowed. "Whyever not? Many is the hand that offers us aide, so we should be the first to help those in need."

Tikva's breath caught in her chest at the simple yet profound statement. "And you have my deepest gratitude. But..." She darted a glance at the other woman, whose face was mostly hidden by a thick veil, with only two jewel-like green eyes showing. "Don't you know who I am?"

The woman barked out a laugh. "Well, of course we do. You're the Unclean Woman of Ptolemais."

If the woman had punched her in the stomach, Tikva could not have been any more surprised at hearing the designation with her own ears. She'd heard whispers, of course, as she scuttled by with her head down, veering far to the side of the street to allow for those who were offended by her presence to pass. Thanks to her mother's loose-lipped friend Tamar, the constant issue of blood from her body was common knowledge. But to have someone look her full in the face and call her such a name was devastating.

"Now," said the woman, tutting at her stricken expression, "don't go being offended by words, my dear. For that is what they are, just words. Levon there"—she pointed at the shorter man, whose one eye was milky white—"they call him One-Eye. Which, of course, he is." She guffawed at her own jest. "And my man, Hiram"—she gestured to the larger man—"sometimes they jest about his toothlessness and other times about the strange noises he makes with the ones he has."

Hiram grinned at Tikva and whistled through the gaps in his mouth. A smile ticked at the corner of Tikva's lips, for the big man's eyes twinkled with mirth.

"I have no problems with my person," said the woman. "But folks that have known me for years are well aware that I had to sell my body after my first man died, not that I had much of a choice with two babies suckling at the time." She spoke without apology. "So you can imagine the words I've had flung my way. And Na'ami"—she turned a gentle smile on the other woman in their party, her brash tone warming—"if anyone understands being called unclean, it's my daughter."

With a linen-wrapped hand, Na'ami slipped her veil down to reveal the scaly, leprous lesions that had overtaken the majority of her face. Although it was by far the most painful sight Tikva had ever seen, the clear, sea-green eyes that stared back at her were full of something she'd never seen before in a stranger. Understanding.

Yes, the others might be outcasts because of their deformities or their sad pasts, but Na'ami knew what it was like to be forced to cross the street in order to avoid people's touch. By law, she even must loudly declare herself to be unclean within a crowd so as not to accidentally taint someone else with the brush of her hand. She knew what it was like to feel as though her body were consuming itself and wish that it all might just end so she could be at peace.

A profound silence moved between Tikva and Na'ami in the breadth of only a few moments, a shared empathy and a connection born of pain. But just as swiftly, Na'ami replaced the veil and the connection was severed.

"Levon is not his eye," said the older woman. "Hiram is not his teeth. Na'ami is not her skin. I am not my past. Those are only things that will pass away, never to be thought of in the world to come."

How could such depth of wisdom come from the mouth of a woman who unabashedly proclaimed herself to have once lived as a prostitute? Someone whom most people would blame for her daughter's affliction?

The woman moved within arm's length of Tikva, her tone now as gentle as it had been when speaking of Na'ami. "I know you hurt, sweet girl," she said and then lifted her dirty palms to cup Tikva's tear-stained cheeks. "But you, my dear, are not your poor, bleeding womb."

A sob broke from Tikva's mouth and, regardless that the woman's threadbare clothes smelled of sweat and filth, she laid her head on her shoulder and wept.

◆

Tikva discovered that the beggar-woman upon whose shoulder she'd cried was called Chavah, just like the first woman in the Garden of Eden, in whose womb all human life was cradled at the very beginning. Something about the words Chavah had offered Tikva seemed to promise a new beginning as well.

After her tears had dried and she'd apologized for her outburst, the group insisted on accompanying her to the gates of the city, from where they would travel on.

Hiram brushed away Tikva's attempt to push the cart and, with his toothless grin, hefted the handles with ease, taking care to avoid the deepest ruts so as to not damage the pottery any further.

"Where are the four of you going?" Tikva asked.

"Capernaum," said Chavah.

"So far? Is that not near the Sea of Kinneret in Galilee?"

"That it is," she said. "A journey of many days, to be sure."

"What would possess you to walk so far?" asked Tikva.

"We search for the rabbi," she replied.

"Which rabbi?"

"Haven't you heard? A Galilean has arisen as a great healer in the past few months. The talk of it is all over the land."

Tikva swallowed the bone-weary sigh that threatened to erupt from her mouth. More talk of healers. More false claims. She hated to see these kind people be taken in by yet another charlatan claiming to wield the powers of the Almighty.

"Please," she said, "listen to me. I've been to more than my fair share of healers over these past years, so I know of what I speak."

Whenever Helena had heard talk of one of these purported healers traveling in the area, she'd taken yet another portion of their meager earnings to bribe them to come lay hands on Tikva, to sing their healing songs and chant their healing chants over her, or to anoint her head with all manner of oils. And just as with all the physicians and midwives, nothing had come of it. Nothing ever would.

"These men and women simply prey on well-meaning and hopeful people like yourselves," she continued. "Hawking their miracle cures or their supposed secret knowledge before disappearing, never to reap the consequences of the broken promises they've left in their wake."

"And I would agree with you in most cases," said Chavah. "But this rabbi is not a charlatan."

The Healer's Touch: Tikva's Story

Tikva shook her head, desperate to make them understand. "He is just like all the rest. He will take whatever coins you have in your hand and leave you with nothing but rocks to eat."

"But that is just the thing. He takes nothing." Confusion furrowed her forehead.

"Yes, I would agree that men who sell their miracles are nothing but thieves, but this man, this Rabbi Yeshua, does not take even a mite from anyone. He does not demand coin in trade for healing."

"I don't understand," said Tikva.

"Neither do we understand it. But we have heard fantastic things, Tikva. One man we met in the market at Ptolemais claimed to have a sister who attended a wedding where this rabbi was and he turned huge pots of water into wine!" Chavah's eyes sparkled with delight. "The sister said it was the best wine anyone had ever put to their lips."

"Another story tells of a young boy practically leaping from his sickbed," said Hiram. "No fever in sight. And at the very hour Rabbi Yeshua prophesied of his healing!"

"These do sound like lovely stories," said Tikva, before they could provide her with more tales. "But that is what they are, my friends. Stories. You will likely spend days and days walking to Capernaum and discover that he, and the men he pays to assist in his tricks, have melted into the wind."

Tikva sighed as the five of them stopped walking, having arrived at the crossroads outside Ptolemais. "I above all others understand what it is like to wish for lasting change. I've laid out my hopes time and again, only to have them trampled into dust."

Chavah regarded her with compassion. "Yes, I can see that in your eyes. But what if—"

"No," interrupted Tikva. "I have no more room for what-ifs. I wasted all of them on things that never came to pass. I choose to hold on to what I have for the time I have left, not waste it on worthless hopes."

"We don't expect this Yeshua to grow new teeth in Hiram's head. Or replace the eye that clouded over when Levon was just a boy. And he certainly cannot restore the years the locusts consumed in my life. But if there is any chance that he can heal my girl…" Chavah's voice warbled as she smiled at Na'ami with an expression of fierce devotion. "Then I will walk any distance and turn over my very soul to this Yeshua of Nazareth. I believe that Adonai has finally heard my prayers."

Defeated by their persistence, Tikva nodded in understanding. Who was she to quash the hopes of these beggars? What else did they possess other than the hope that a kind person might drop a coin into their palms? They could certainly beg in Galilee just as well as they could here. She only prayed that this rabbi of theirs might not strip them of what remained of their dignity, the way the Greek physician had done to her.

She forced a smile. "Then go, and may Adonai cause your path to be smooth before you."

"You will not consider coming with us?" asked Chavah. "Perhaps this Yeshua might—"

The Healer's Touch: Tikva's Story

Tikva lifted a palm to halt the half-constructed sentence. She could not afford the thought to become a fully spoken one, nor to gain any purchase on her imagination.

"I thank you again for coming to my rescue, and for your kind words," she said to Chavah with sincere gratitude, for she'd truly felt a shift within her soul when Chavah had declared that her broken womb was not the sum total of her being. "But I must get these pots to my mother-in-law. She'll be worrying over my tardiness."

Although it seemed as though Chavah might have more to say, Tikva fixed a determined expression on her face. She would never again allow some roving healer with greedy palms to examine her body, not that she would have anything to trade for healing if she wanted to. It was all gone.

With words of peace and blessing, the beggars took their leave of her, veering toward the east and Galilee. She watched them walk away, Hiram and Levon lumbering along ahead of the females, Chavah with her arm hooked in the elbow of her precious daughter.

Only Na'ami looked back, her large green eyes meeting Tikva's again, and in the most secret part of her heart, Tikva hoped, for Na'ami's sake, that she was wrong.

CHAPTER TWELVE

◆

"I don't know why this piece has not sold yet," said Helena as she placed the delicate vase in the bed of the cart, tucking straw around the long neck to prevent it from shifting during the return to Simcha's house.

"It is lovely," said Tikva, peeking around the curtain at the back of the pottery stall. Watching Helena repack all the unsold goods in the wagon and not being able to help was one of the most frustrating parts of her day. But although the majority of people who flooded into the market would not care if her unclean hands touched their pots or jars or oil lamps, there were always those few like the women from a few weeks ago, who were offended by her mere presence, let alone her touch, and they could not chance losing business because of it. And so, as she did every day, Tikva stayed hidden while Helena worked, and pressed down the guilt to the best of her ability.

"It is a beautiful creation," said her mother-in-law. "At least four customers commented on the color of the glaze, but none so much as gave me an offer. Although perhaps—" Helena darted a glance at Tikva and then shook her head, turning back to lift another of the unsold pieces from the table and press it securely into the straw.

"Perhaps what?" Tikva asked, distracted by the sight of a little girl, probably one of the children of a merchant, who'd noticed Tikva peeking around the curtain and was giggling and waving at her.

"Oh"—Helena swiped her palm through the air—"just some talk in the market."

The child forgotten, Tikva's defenses roared to life. "Is Medad insulting Simcha's work again?" Their closest competitor always did his best to entice customers to his cheap goods, but since Helena had dressed down the unscrupulous dealer when last year he'd gone so far as to mock Simcha's work as that of a crippled amateur, he'd not dared to raise one word against them.

"No, no. It's nothing like that. Just…goings on. Rumors." Helena's lips pulled into a tight smile that Tikva did not for one moment believe.

"Tell me," she said, perplexed by Helena's awkward movements and avoidance of her gaze. "Will these rumors cut into our sales? Simcha was hoping to take on an apprentice soon."

"It has nothing to do with the pottery, daughter. I…I vowed to not raise the subject with you again, and I am trying to honor that promise."

A prickle of unease raised the hair on Tikva's neck. The only promise her mother-in-law had made recently was to avoid all mention of what she'd experienced in Caesarea, and anything else related to her condition.

But Helena seemed so on edge, her shoulders taut and high as she went about her work and her mouth pursed as if attempting to keep whatever was inside from bursting free.

Tikva released a resigned sigh. "Tell me."

Helena wrung her hands together and surveyed Tikva's countenance, likely determining whether whatever she had to say was worth upsetting her again. "I want to fulfill my vow, Tikva. I truly do, but after today...after what I said before, I don't know that I can."

Alarm began to thrum in Tikva's chest. She hadn't seen Helena this reluctant to speak with her since the day she'd announced that she would be forced to sell off her lovely home to pay her husband's debts.

"Go on," Tikva urged. "Whatever you have to say, I will not be angry. I promise."

"You know I love you," said Helena, coming around the curtain to face Tikva straight on. "Asa was my only child, as you know. A miracle in a long line of failed births."

She did know this. Helena had shared her own pain years ago when Tikva's babe first died.

"And when you married my son I was happy, because you seemed a sweet child, if a little flighty." A teasing grin tilted her mouth before it melted away. "But our hearts were bound together by our tragedy, weren't they?"

Tikva's eyes misted, for she'd often thought the same thing. "Without you I would not be alive," she whispered.

"I think, perhaps, the same might be said for me," said her mother-in-law. "I know that I pushed too many midwives on you in the first years, Tikva, and too many men who called themselves physicians, but I think concentrating on finding a solution to your problem kept my mind off my own wounds.

And then, of course, working here in the marketplace has been a wonderful occupation for my mind as well. It, too, has given me a renewed purpose, a sense of satisfaction that truly was missing even in my life before."

Again, Tikva felt the same way. She'd abhorred sitting around the lovely villa with nothing to occupy her hands back then. And realizing that the many friends she'd once had thought nothing of tossing her to the side once she was deemed untouchable made her cherish the friendships with Helena, Simcha, and Adina all the more.

"But I failed you when I pushed you to go to that Greek physician—" Helena raised a staying hand when Tikva tried to interrupt. "No. Hear me out, please. That ill-conceived plan hurt you, both your body and your soul." Tears glittered in the older woman's blue eyes. "I'd thought perhaps medicine from the land of my birth, medicine blessed by the gods of that place, might be the solution, since I'd decided the God of this land must not have enough power to heal you."

The confession wounded Tikva, since the expression on her mother-in-law's face made it clear that she'd known all along that the Greek physician's home was nothing more than a temple to Asclepius.

Tikva had already suspected as much, so she simply said, "I forgive you."

Helena nodded her gratitude, one tear trailing down to her quivering chin. "When I married Nachman I found no issue joining myself to your people's God. I loved him, so I converted without truly understanding, and I kept your laws and remained faithful until he died. But I meant what I said that last day we argued over going to the synagogue."

Tikva remembered her words well: "...*that vow is on the bottom of the sea, along with my husband and my son. Unless Adonai raises the dead to life, that is where it will stay.*"

A slow smile began to grow on Helena's face. "But he did it, Tikva. He raised the dead to life."

"I–I don't understand." Tikva sank down to settle on a stool.

"There have been rumors floating around in the market for months, things I gave little credence to—something about a Galilean claiming to be some sort of healer."

Immediately Tikva remembered the morning a few weeks ago when she'd crossed paths with those four beggars. They too had spoken of a Galilean healer.

"There have been many who claimed such things, Helena," she said, using the same argument she had with Chavah. "You, of all people, know this."

"Of course. Wherever there is sickness and hurt, there will be those who claim they can repair such things. But this man, Tikva." She shook her head in disbelief. "You cannot imagine the things that have been told of him."

Tikva remembered the story of the water turned to wine and the boy rising from his sickbed with no sign of fever, but gave no indication that she also had heard such tales.

"It is said," continued Helena, "that large crowds have begun to follow him wherever he goes, coming from all over the land and beyond to hear the man speak and to come into his presence. The lame. The blind. Those twisted of mind. The lepers. All hoping for a miracle."

Just as Tikva's four new friends had been doing. Walking nearly the breadth of the land to find this mysterious rabbi.

"I largely ignored the talk, as I normally do. So many fantastical tales are spun by the men who arrive in port that one must choose sparingly what to believe. But today, Tikva. Today Adonai opened my eyes." Tikva held her breath as Helena brushed her fingers over her own trembling lips. "The dead have been raised to life."

Profound confusion swallowed up any response Tikva might have had.

"I probably would have brushed aside the story," Helena said, "had I not spoken to a man who was there. The very one responsible for bringing the story to the market in the first place. He is a traveling merchant, one who moves back and forth between a few of the villages in the area around the Sea of Kinneret and the port here. He was in the town of Nain when this traveling rabbi came through, a large group of hangers-on in his wake. A funeral procession was moving through town, that of a young man who'd died just that morning. His poor mother," she said, her voice thick with empathy, "was heartbroken. Barely able to walk to the burial grounds outside the town, as if every bone in her body were liquefied with grief."

Tikva knew the feeling all too well. She'd not been aware of anything the day they'd buried her child. She hadn't gotten to accompany her son's tiny body to the grave and grieved it every day.

"But this rabbi, daughter—he could have walked on, gone about his journey, but instead he approached the widow, speaking to her in such low tones that only those closest to him could divine the words. Then to the surprise of all gathered there, both the mourners and his flock of followers, he walked over to the body and told the young man to rise."

A rush of overwhelming sensation flooded through Tikva. Surely this story was a fabrication, but as Helena paused to take a breath and wipe her face, anticipation began to thrum in Tikva's limbs.

"And?" she prompted.

"And the corpse began to move."

Glad for the solid stool beneath her, Tikva stared at her mother-in-law, trying to gauge whether she actually believed what she was hearing.

"The merchant told me that the entire valley seemed to erupt. Panic. Wails. Some ran to the hills in terror. Many dropped to their knees in worship. But within only a few moments, the young man had been removed from his burial clothes and was walking around in full view of everyone."

"He must have been merely sleeping, a false death," Tikva countered.

"This merchant swears it was not, that a local physician declared his heart to be still, his skin cold, and the stiffness already beginning to lock his bones in place when he'd been discovered motionless in his bed that morning. No, Tikva. This young man was raised from the dead. And what is more, this Rabbi Yeshua, as he is called, made it clear that the miracle was only to be attributed to the power of God, not by the means of any mortal flesh. It was not my gods that did this, daughter. Adonai raised the boy to life, through this rabbi."

Tikva jolted to her feet and took a few steps backward, knowing exactly what would come next from her mother-in-law's lips.

"And if this man wields a divine power that can raise the dead to life—then surely he can heal you."

CHAPTER THIRTEEN

Ankle deep in the river, Adina plunged her hands into the water. "I found more!" she called, drawing out a large handful of soupy muck then giggling as she squished the lump in her fist to ensure that she had indeed found a deposit of clay. This spot on the river, where the water swirled into slow-moving eddies, was the most prolific source of fine clay Simcha had found in years. Tikva hoped that none of the other potters in Ptolemais would discover such a profitable secret.

Simcha limped heavily over to his daughter to affirm her discovery. Even after twelve years of watching him struggle against his twisted leg, it still astounded Tikva that he could move as quickly as he could without his wooden crutch, which was impossible to use on the spongy riverbank.

"Excellent!" he said, gifting his daughter an adoring smile. "You always find the best clay, little bird."

Tikva never failed to enjoy the weekly excursion to the river to gather clay, even though digging out the gluey masses and then spending hours stirring and filtering the mess was a taxing endeavor. But being out under the blue sky and listening to the birdsong and the rush of the river just before it pushed out to sea did much to soothe her turbulent soul.

However, today a wave of exhaustion had stripped most of the usual joy she felt at working alongside Simcha, Adina, and Helena at the river. She'd not yet told Helena, but the flow of blood for the past four mornings had been almost twice what it was before the Greek physician touched her body. Not only had the man not healed her, it seemed he'd made her worse than before.

Tikva breathed deeply to infuse herself with fresh air, hoping the tang of the sea salt on the breeze might revive her weary mind and body. She slowly poured a bowlful of muddy water into a tightly woven sack that Simcha had tied onto a low tree branch—the first step in filtering out the sand and grit from what would eventually become fine-quality clay for Simcha's work.

Beside her, Helena stirred another large vessel, preparing the slurry for Tikva to filter as Simcha and Adina collected the next batch from the riverbed. The four of them had nearly perfected their process over the years and were able to harvest just enough clay for Simcha to create a week's worth of pottery.

As she leaned down to scoop another bowlful of water, a rush of dizziness roared through Tikva's head. Her limbs feeling suddenly far too heavy, she dropped the bowl in the jar and reached for the tree branch, only to miss and find herself slumping to the ground, her cheek landing in the mucky mess beneath her filtering bag.

Half aware, Tikva heard Helena cry out for Simcha, and Adina call out her name, but her eyelids refused to stay open, so she closed them and gave in to the blessed rest.

"…this rabbi. It is her last chance, I fear," said Helena.

"I might have to agree with you," said Simcha. "Although I don't know how we can get her to Capernaum when she is so weak."

"I know a way," said Helena.

"No," mumbled Tikva as her mouth began to catch up with her mind. "There is no use."

Her eyes fluttered open, and she realized that Simcha had her propped up against his chest and was looking down on her with something akin to panic in his brown eyes. She'd not been this close to a man since Asa, and the proximity brought her back to full consciousness. She struggled against him, attempting to sit upright, but his strong arms held her tight.

"You are not ready yet, Tikva," he said, the words gentle but firm. "Just rest for a while. I have you."

Although flushed with embarrassment, both from the faint and from how wonderful it felt to be embraced like this, she acquiesced. The last thing she wanted was to be helpless on the ground once again.

"I am not going to that healer," she said. "I have had enough of false hopes. If this is my time to pass into the world to come, then it is my time."

Simcha's jaw worked, and his eyes narrowed. "And so you will give up then? When such miracles are happening in Israel? When you have the chance to be freed from this prison?"

The Healer's Touch: Tikva's Story

Tikva was startled by his vehemence. "So you too believe that this rabbi is who he claims to be?"

"I don't know for sure, of course. But even I, locked as I am in my workshop most of the time, have heard the things he's been purported to do. I don't know how they could all be lies when it seems as though everything he's done has been in full view of a crowd of people."

"That is hard to dismiss, daughter," said Helena. "I know you have your doubts. But Tikva, he raised a man from the dead!"

"I don't believe such a thing really happened. It simply cannot be," said Tikva. "You are placing your hopes on a foundation of mist. No, I am done with this fight. Please, just let me die in peace."

Adina's sob rent through the silence. "How can you say such things? You would leave us? You would leave *me* when you have the chance to be healed by this rabbi? We need you, Tikva. I need you." Tears ran down her muddy cheeks, dripping off her chin in quick succession.

The girl's distress speared Tikva through. "I don't want to die, sweet girl. But this sickness is too strong. I cannot fight against it anymore. I am too tired."

"Then let us fight it with you," she said. "You have helped us all these years, now it is time for us to help you."

The desperate plea on Adina's precious face was too much for Tikva to guard against. How could she possibly refuse this child anything?

She closed her eyes, feeling Simcha's steady heartbeat against her cheek. "Please," he said, and she felt the rumble of his voice through his chest. "She is right. We all need you." Then in a whisper he added, "I need you."

The undercurrent of his tender words made her catch her breath, and although she dare not cling to them, they pushed past her reservations. Resigned, she nodded and heard all three of her companions sigh in victory.

"Good," said Helena. "Now, for my plan. I've been talking with my friends Meira and Zuri. They do a regular trading run to Galilee twice a year, and they are leaving in only one week. They gave Tikva and me permission to ride along with the caravan. We can sell some pottery along the way whenever we pass through villages, so we will have some money for food and essentials. It may take some time, but it sounds as though Rabbi Yeshua returns to Capernaum often, so one way or the other, we will find him."

"I cannot allow the two of you to go alone," said Simcha. "If I'd known you were going to Caesarea without me last month, especially to go to some heathen physician, I would have stopped you."

Helena looked sufficiently chagrined by his pointed stare. "Yes," she said. "And you would have been right to do so. I wish I'd never pressed her to go." She wrung her hands at her waist. "Obviously it has done much more harm than good."

"We will talk no more of it," said Simcha. "What's done is done. But I think it best if I go with Tikva. Helena, you can stay with Adina. She's old enough now to help you with the pottery stall while we are gone."

"Oh yes!" declared Adina with a clap of her muddy hands, all sorrow washed away by the prospect of a new responsibility. "I would love to help you!"

"I cannot ask you to leave your workshop," said Tikva.

"You are not asking," he said, his tone brooking no argument. "And I have plenty of inventory for Helena to sell over the next month or so, especially if I build up extra stock over the next few days."

"But is it seemly for the two of us to travel together to Capernaum?" asked Tikva.

"You won't be alone. There are at least three other women traveling with the caravan. You'll never have cause to be without others to witness your upright behavior."

"These traders, they know who I am?" she asked. "They would tolerate my presence among them?"

"They are Phoenicians. They do not care who you are, nor what ails you." Helena shrugged. "Besides, they owe me a favor. A large one."

Tikva sighed, knowing that for every argument she might have, Helena already had an answer prepared. "Well, if we only have a few days to prepare for this journey, I'd best continue filtering this clay."

"Are you certain you have the strength?" asked Simcha, concern twisting his brow. "The three of us are plenty able to finish this job if you would like to return home and rest some more."

"I have enough for today," said Tikva, and willed her body to believe it. "And that will have to be sufficient for now."

With seeming great reluctance, Simcha allowed her to push out of his arms and stand, but she immediately missed the sensation of being held close by someone who genuinely cared for her. Ignoring the whisper of hope's wings against her heart, she retrieved the bowl she'd lost in the mucky water and set her mind to her task.

CHAPTER FOURTEEN

✦

The endless days of bumping along in the back of the donkey cart were taking a toll on Tikva. She glanced over at Simcha, who hobbled along beside the cart on his crutch with amazing dexterity. Her body had refused to allow her to walk more than an hour or so each day, so she'd been forced to endure the journey from Caesarea nestled between bundles of foreign fabrics, jars of oil from Cyrus, and stacks of pottery. Thankfully, Meira and Zuri, along with the other traders who made up this small caravan, had been kind enough to search out the smoothest routes possible between the numerous villages they traveled through. But still, her weary body was covered in bruises from the many jolting ruts along the way.

"Does it not hurt?" she asked Simcha, gesturing toward his twisted leg. "After so much walking?"

"No. It has never been painful, only a frustration."

Regardless that he seemed unaffected by the long journey on foot, she was glad that their traveling companions had declared that they would arrive in Capernaum just before nightfall and finally, they all could rest.

"It always amazed me," she murmured.

"What?"

"How quick you were on that crutch. Even when you were a boy."

A satisfied smile curved his lips. "You remember me as a boy?"

"Of course I do. It used to make me so sad."

"Don't think on it. I was born with my leg twisted, it really does not hurt me. It never has."

"No, it used to make me sad that the other children excluded you."

His smile melted. "Oh. Yes, well, of course that was hurtful."

"I am sorry."

"For what?"

"That I never asked you to play with us. That I was not brave enough to reach out, or even speak to you."

"There is nothing to forgive, Tikva." The gentle expression on Simcha's face sent another pang of guilt through her. "You were a child and knew no better."

"I did," she said. "I saw the longing on your face as you watched us. I should have said something to my cousins. Or at least spoken to you."

"Do you know what I remember of you?" His brows lifted with his smile.

"I am not certain that I want to know," she said.

"I remember the sound of your laughter. Whenever I would watch you all playing together, your laugh was so bright and lovely that I was drawn to it. It reminded me of a sparrow warbling in a tree."

Tikva's cheeks warmed at the compliment.

"And there was one time, just before I was sent to Alexandria, that your cousin fell and scraped her knees near the synagogue. You were so concerned about her, I even think you began crying yourself...." His voice melted away.

"I remember that," she said, although she'd not known that Simcha had witnessed the instance.

"You may not have spoken to me then, Tikva, but I saw your kindness. Your compassion. I knew that if things were different, we would have been friends."

If only things *had* been different, she thought. If only she'd known that it would not be her cousins, or any of the others whom she called friends standing by her side when her life was ripped from her hands, but this gentle man who remained steadfast through it all, although he had no cause to do so. How different would life have been if she'd stepped past the line made by ungracious hearts and sought out his friendship earlier in life? Or what if he had never been an outcast in the first place?

A question bubbled to her lips, spilling free before she was able to wrangle it. "What if you'd not been born with twisted limbs?" Horrified by her rudeness, she immediately lifted a palm to stop his answer. "Forgive me, that was—"

"No," said Simcha, unperturbed. "It's a fair question. I don't mind answering what might have been." His gaze glided to the far horizon, where Tikva could make out the smallest glimpse of water between two distant hills, their destination finally within sight after days and days of traveling.

"I have asked this of myself, of course. Many times. What would my life be if I had the ability to walk without a crutch? If

I could have scurried about town and played with you and your friends? If instead of puttering about in the mud I could have gone to sea like my older brothers, seen the world, and explored foreign ports? What if," he continued, "I was not forced to marry my cousin, who, although she was generally kind, merely tolerated me and resented my limitations?"

A wave of sadness crashed over Tikva. She'd not known much of Rachel, and he'd spoken nothing against the woman, but how could anyone merely tolerate Simcha? He was everything good and kind and steady, he was a father who doted on his child, he reached out a hand to two widows and offered them a way to sustain themselves when they had nothing left. The hand and leg he'd been born with changed none of those things, and, in fact, made them even more worthy of praise.

"And yet," he continued, "no matter how many times I ask myself all of these questions, I only come to one conclusion. It doesn't matter, because I would not change a thing."

"You wouldn't?"

"No, Tikva. Don't you see? If I had not been born with twisted limbs I would not have spent hour upon hour upon hour watching my abba craft pottery with an expert hand. I'd likely have been out with my brothers playing swords and watching the ships glide in and out of port and dreaming of the day when I could step foot on deck and disappear over the horizon. My brothers hated the pottery. Couldn't stand the idea of spending their lives at the wheel. But I cannot imagine my life *without* the turning of that stone beneath my foot. And I would trade nothing for the time I had in Alexandria learning from my uncles and discovering the privilege it is to transform a lump of clay into something useful, something beautiful." A smile quirked on his lips. "It almost makes me feel at one with the Creator who formed Adam from the dust of the ground."

Tikva's breath was trapped within her lungs as he spoke, the fervor of his speech filling her with some unnamed emotion.

"And no matter that Rachel held little affection in her heart for me," he said, his voice growing stronger. "And resented the only life I was able to provide her with. She gave me the best gift I could ever ask for—Adina. And for her I would change nothing in my life. Every wound, every sneering stranger, every frustration was worth the path I took, for her."

The sliver of water Tikva had sighted in the east widened into a grand vista of a silver lake that stretched from one end of the valley to the other. Considering the unknowns that awaited her down there, she asked one more question of this man who'd done more for her than any of her own blood relations combined and who deserved more than she could ever hope to repay.

"And if this rabbi is who he claims to be, if he can truly heal. What if…" She took in a shuddering breath. "What if he could heal you too?"

Simcha was silent for a long while, his eyes also on the distant shore, where a number of towns were already visible in the fast advancing dusk. A few lights already shone from windows to welcome them to the wide and fertile valley, where either astounding miracles or crushed dreams awaited them.

"It still would change nothing," he said. "I am more than content with my life. Between Adina and my pottery, I have everything I need, and indeed, have much for which to rejoice. As for what I want..." His eyes turned back to Tikva, holding her captive for a breathless moment as he seemed to study her face the way she'd seen discerning customers study one of his more beautiful vases at the market stall. "There is only one more thing I could ever hope to ask for. I hoped for it, years ago, but it was not meant to be then. Perhaps...perhaps if this Rabbi Yeshua is who he says he is, the desire of my heart might yet be mine."

As a few sprinkles of rain tapped against her overheated cheeks, Tikva's own heart pounded out an unfamiliar rhythm. Was he implying what she thought? That he still wanted to marry her? He'd never in all these years even hinted at such a thing again, even though they worked together day after day. Had she been blind to the reflection of her own futile imaginings in Simcha's warm brown eyes?

A gust of wind blew off her head scarf as Zuri called out for the group to stop and take shelter from the rain. It seemed that, although Capernaum was well within sight now, they would have to wait until the morning to begin their search for the man who might change everything, for both of them.

CHAPTER FIFTEEN

When their little group entered Capernaum early the next morning, Tikva was not surprised that the townspeople were busy setting things to rights after the sudden violent storm that had swirled over the Galilee like a thick pot of stew for what seemed like hours.

Even Meira and Zuri had sustained a loss, as one of their mules had panicked in the throes of the tempest and somehow escaped his moorings to run off. Therefore, since a second wagon had to be hooked behind their remaining mule, Tikva had been forced to walk the last two hours to Capernaum, her body screaming for rest by the time they set foot in the lakeside town.

A few fishing vessels bobbed along the shoreline, one that looked to have sacrificed its mast to the winds last night. The town itself was built primarily of the local basalt, its gray-bricked homes and businesses nearly blending into the silver-shadowed water at its back.

Now having seen many of the rough-hewn farm villages that dotted the countryside on their way through the land, Tikva appreciated the solidity of Capernaum, its permanence seemingly etched into the earth with thick lines. The synagogue stood with proud grace at the center of town, a testament to the longevity of the words contained within its walls.

Leaving their wagons just outside the town in the care of their friends, Meira and Zuri headed directly to the market to search out a spot to display the imported goods they'd carried from Ptolemais. Since Simcha had parted with them, determined to search out a local potter, Tikva followed the couple through the market, where vendors were just beginning to lay out their wares and prepare for the day, glad that no one in Capernaum knew her. The simple act of walking among a crowd without being pointed out as unclean or enduring a wake of whispers on the street gave her a sense of freedom she'd not enjoyed for twelve years.

The stalls and produce wagons stationed along the streets were not nearly as numerous as in Ptolemais, but since Capernaum was located on a main trade road, business was still bustling. The smell of fresh fish rose above all other aromas in the town, and it seemed as though a number of fishermen had just returned with their night's catch, busy as they were laying out their silver-scaled goods on tables and calling out their offerings to entice customers.

Except for the crush of bodies jammed into the market this morning, nothing in Capernaum seemed out of the ordinary. Had everyone been mistaken about this being the place this mysterious rabbi lived? She saw no multitude gathered in this town. No roiling, pressing mass of people calling out for healing the way she'd imagined. Was this truly a place of miracles? Or just another town blinded by a charlatan who'd already disappeared with their shekels?

"Did you see that storm?" asked one of the wine merchants Meira had been speaking with. "I've never seen its like, and I've lived on this shore for forty-three years." He scratched his forehead with two grape-stained fingers.

"We'd not quite made it into Capernaum by the time the winds began to stir," said Meira. "We were camped along the road well before the clouds opened."

"Then you did not see it end?" asked the man, his eyes wide.

Meira's brows furrowed. "No. We took shelter beneath our wagons during the worst of it."

"Well, now. That's just the thing," said the wine merchant. "Storms are no new thing around here. A squall kicks up every now and then over the Kinneret, but it's rare that any have such power. And there was no warning. The sky was gray to be sure, a bit of rain expected. But these clouds built so quickly that many of the fishermen were caught unaware. Such churning," he said with an air of incredulity. "At least three boats that I know of have gone missing."

"How awful," said Meira. "And the men lost too?"

"That they were," said the merchant. "Not all from this town, but we mourn them all the same."

"What made the end of this storm any different from the others you've experienced?" asked Meira.

"Well now, the wind had been howling for a while, and the waters were almost completely white with waves, but then, without any warning, it stopped."

"It stopped?"

"Like a flame being snuffed out." He pinched two fingers together with a whistling gust of air through his lips. "Within only a few moments the water was still as glass. No wind. No rain. No waves."

"How odd," said Meira.

"That it was," said the merchant. He learned toward Meira. "Some say it was *him*."

"Him?"

"That rabbi. Yeshua."

Meira stared at the man for a few moments before letting a burst of laughter free. "A man stopped a storm? I've heard of miracle healings and such by this rabbi." She glanced back at Tikva. "But it is the gods who control the heavens. Not any man."

"Perhaps not," said the merchant. "But perhaps you should save your judgments until he returns. This place has seen things…." He shook his head. "Things that have no explanation at all."

A burst of courage came from Tikva's lips. "When will he return? The rabbi."

His perusal of her face was unnerving, so she pulled the veil tighter across her chin. "Your guess would be the same as mine, my dear. He comes and goes when he pleases. But they left in a boat last night, headed for the other side, I believe. If he and his men survived that storm, they might be over there for a few days. Or he may go somewhere else, and then who knows when he might return? At least the crowd that swarms the town whenever he is present has moved off into the countryside."

"Is that not a good thing for the merchants here?" asked Meira.

"Depends on what you mean by a good thing. To be sure business rises when they come, which of course is welcome. But those of us who are local tire easily of our town being overrun. They sleep in the alleys, they fill the streets to overflowing, and many of them are beggars, so their hands are ever lifted. We tire of the whole thing and wish this rabbi would just move along for good."

"Then you don't *actually* believe he's performing miracles?" asked Tikva.

The man shrugged. "Perhaps. Perhaps not. I am still undecided on the entire matter. But if things continue this way, the Romans might have something to say about it. The rabbis here certainly do."

Disheartened, Tikva thanked the man for his help and then silently followed Meira as she conversed with a few other merchants before rejoining her husband and heading back to their wagons.

Simcha had indeed found a potter, a kind man who'd been impressed by his work and offered to sell the rest of his stock at his stall in exchange for a portion of the profits. At least they would have enough money to eat for the next few days. But if this healing rabbi tarried more than a week, they might be forced to return with Meira and Zuri with nothing more to show for their journey than a few shekels.

As they headed to the northern edge of town, toward the house of the potter, who'd also offered their group the use of his small courtyard during their stay, Tikva's gaze was drawn to the far shore of the Kinneret, where, according to the wine merchant, Yeshua and his followers had been heading when they left to fish the prior evening. A few boats were out there now, bobbing gently on the surface of the water that had, if the merchant was to be believed, been whipped into a frenzy. Had Yeshua and his followers also been swallowed by the waves last night? Or could she dare to believe that, like the rumors suggested, the rabbi's powers were not limited to healing? She remembered well the stories of the Great Exodus from Egypt, when her forefathers walked through the depths of the sea. Would a man sent from Adonai to heal allow him such control over wind and waves? She shook her head at the thought, reminding herself that she was here to appease Helena, Simcha, and Adina. She could not allow her hopes to be inflated by such foolish notions.

"Tikva!" a voice called out.

Disoriented by the sound of her name being shouted in the midst of an unfamiliar town, she halted for a moment and looked about, briefly searching the faces of the people passing by them on the road. Not seeing anyone she knew, and thinking perhaps she'd imagined the voice, she pressed onward to catch up with the wagon.

"Tikva! Stop!" said the voice again, from closer this time.

Simcha too had heard the summons now and called out for Meira and Zuri to halt the caravan's progress. Turning around, Tikva watched in confusion as a young woman approached, her hand upraised in greeting. Although the girl was lovely and the expression on her face indicated pleasure at coming across Tikva, she was completely unfamiliar.

"It *is* you," said the young woman with a broad smile. "My mother insisted it was so."

"I'm sorry," said Tikva. "I don't...who are you?"

The young woman's smile grew impossibly large. "I can understand why you might be confused," she said. "Perhaps if I do this—" She lifted the edge of her tattered head scarf and brought it across her mouth and nose, until just her eyes were visible in the gap.

Tikva peered at her, her jaw going slack as she realized that indeed, she did recognize the sea-colored eyes that sparkled at her with a mixture of delight and anticipation. Those eyes had met hers on the road outside Ptolemais, when four threadbare beggars had stopped to give her aid.

"Na'ami?"

CHAPTER SIXTEEN

❖

Tikva could not reconcile that the face she saw before her was the same one she'd beheld back in Ptolemais. There was no trace of disease, no scars, nothing at all to indicate that this young woman had once been afflicted by leprosy.

"But...how could this be?" asked Tikva, her gaze traveling over the woman's smooth, clear skin and the arms and hands that were no longer wrapped in protective linen. Na'ami was whole. And what was more, because of it, she would no longer be considered unclean. Was this the work of Yeshua?

"My mother saw you walk by back in the market. She instructed me to follow after you and bring you to her." Without hesitation, Na'ami reached for Tikva's hand. "Come, please. Come with me, and we will break our fasts together. I have much to tell you."

Tikva turned to Simcha. "These people are my friends, and..." She looked back at Na'ami's lovely, expectant face. Chavah's declaration from the day they'd met returned to her mind. *"But if there is any chance that he can heal my girl, then I will walk any distance and turn over my very soul to this Yeshua of Nazareth."*

"They came for the same reason we did," she continued. "And it seems that perhaps...they have already met the rabbi?"

She searched Na'ami's face for the answer, and it came with a brilliant smile and a nod.

With a confused pinch between his brows, Simcha looked between Na'ami and Tikva until understanding seemed to dawn, and his countenance lifted.

Without a word, he went to Zuri, giving him directions to the potter's home with the promise that he and Tikva would meet them there later this afternoon.

Once their group had moved on, Tikva and Simcha followed Na'ami back through Capernaum, winding their way south through the market where the air was now replete with the sounds of bartering and the bleat and bray of livestock.

"Have you been here this entire time?" Tikva asked Na'ami when they'd finally broken free of the crowds.

"We have. My mother refused to stop anywhere along the way, determined as she was to get me before Yeshua."

"So you have seen him then. He really did heal you?"

Na'ami's smile rivaled the golden morning light for radiance. "That he did."

A thousand questions lay heavy on Tikva's tongue, but it seemed as though Na'ami was bent on bringing them to her mother before divulging anything more, urging Tikva and Simcha to follow her down a winding path to the water's edge.

Hiram and Chavah were seated together on the beach, shoulder to shoulder and cross-legged in front of a small fire, Levon sitting across from them. The smell of roasting fish tantalized Tikva's senses as they approached.

As soon as she caught sight of the three of them, Chavah bounced to her feet, her movements far too spry for a woman with a full head of silver.

"Tikva!" she called out and rushed to greet her. "I am so delighted that Na'ami found you. We have plenty of food to share between us."

Enduring a kiss of welcome to her cheek and a strong embrace from the beggar woman, Tikva sputtered out her gratitude for the invitation.

"I am certain you have many questions," said Chavah, with an indulgent smile toward her daughter. "I can imagine the sight of my girl was quite a shock."

"Truthfully, I did not recognize her," said Tikva.

Chavah lifted a hand to stroke Na'ami's cheek, her expression full of delight and awe. "No matter that her beauty was hidden, it was always there, beneath the surface. Yeshua simply allowed the outside of my daughter to match the inside."

Simcha's face was a mask of confusion as his gaze flitted between the three women.

"I met Chavah and Na'ami on the road between your home and the market in Ptolemais," Tikva explained. "At the time Na'ami was afflicted with leprosy. Her entire face was affected by the disease."

"Along with the rest of my body, which I kept hidden beneath linen wraps," Na'ami interjected.

"But"—Tikva gestured to her young friend—"as you can see, she is afflicted no more."

Tikva had wondered whether Simcha truly believed the stories of the rabbi, or if by coming on this journey he'd simply been appeasing Helena and his daughter the way Tikva had. The shock on his face answered the question. He'd had doubts, just as she had, but seeing Na'ami, her green eyes practically shouting with jubilation, Tikva's doubts were well on their way to crumbling into nothing. She suspected Simcha's might be as well.

After being greeted heartily by Hiram, who in spite of Na'ami's miraculous healing still had more gaps than teeth, and Levon, who regarded Simcha warily with his one eye, Tikva and Simcha obeyed Chavah's command to sit by the fire and enjoy the fish she'd prepared.

"So you and your husband have come to meet Yeshua, have you?" asked Chavah.

"Oh, this is not my husband. We are unmarried." A flush of heat came to her cheeks as she realized what she'd said. "That is to say, Simcha is a potter. My mother-in-law and I help in his workshop, and he was kind enough to accompany me here. With a number of other traders, of course. We are not alone."

Amusement danced in Chavah's eyes as Tikva stumbled over her explanation. "There is no need to be embarrassed, my friend. I understand what you mean. And of course you know that I am in no place to judge you or anyone else." She winked.

Remembering that Chavah had admitted to selling her body to feed her children many years ago, Tikva attempted a smile, wondering how she might explain this all to Simcha later and whether he would be upset that she'd befriended beggars such as these. But for now, the mystery of Na'ami's healing won out over any other concerns.

"Please, Chavah," she said, "tell me what all has passed since we took leave of each other on the road."

Chavah handed Tikva and Simcha a roasted fish to share between them, along with a cup of watered-down barley beer.

"We came straight here after we parted ways with you on the road, stopping only a few times along the journey to beg for our bread," she said, unabashed about the way they'd managed to survive. "We arrived only a few days after rumors began of Yeshua raising a young man from the dead."

"We heard the same story, all the way in Ptolemais," said Simcha. "It seems such a fantastic tale traveled quickly throughout the land. But is it true?"

"After what I've seen I believe it," said Chavah, with a grin toward her newly healed daughter. "And there are more than a few of Yeshua's followers who witnessed the miracle. They spoke of watching the still body being carried through the town of Nain. They heard Yeshua speak to the corpse before it began to move. Then they saw the young man unwrapped from his grave clothes and watched as he stood and helped support his overcome mother back to their home in order to celebrate."

The pulse of hope that began when she'd seen Na'ami's clear face with her own eyes swelled at Chavah's defense of the inconceivable story of a man raised from the dead.

"When we discovered that a great crowd had gathered to hear him speak nearby, we followed the flow of bodies." Chavah frowned. "It was difficult, since there are so many people clamoring to follow him and to hear his words. We were pushed to the very back of the multitude, and we could not hear his voice from so great a distance. But word was carried back through the crowd, mouth to ear, mouth to ear until we were able to piece together much of it."

Tikva leaned forward, "What did he say? Did he claim to have some secret knowledge that gives him the power to heal?"

"That I do not know. Mostly he tells stories."

Tikva's brow wrinkled. "Stories?"

Chavah nodded. "Yes. Stories like I've never heard before. Some are understandable. Anyone with a mind to hear can see that he urges us to repent and follow Torah, much as the Pharisees do, although he challenges their traditions more often than not. But even more, there is something to his words." She lifted her eyes to gaze across the water at the opposite shore where the man she spoke of had traveled. "Something I cannot express. Some even say he is the Messiah."

Tikva's jaw gaped as she stared at the woman. "But how can a wandering healer be the one foretold by the prophets? He is no king." Deeply ingrained in her since her earliest memories, the words of the Torah read by her father sprang to mind. The prophecies of Moses. Of Isaiah. And of David. Surely it could not be.

"Does he speak of driving the Romans from the land?" Simcha asked.

"Not that I have heard," said Chavah.

A shadow moved across Simcha's features. "Then surely he is not the One we await."

"You have not met him," said Na'ami. "You did not look into his eyes, nor hear his words with your ears. I don't know anything about what will happen with the Romans, nor anything else, but I do know Adonai Himself sent this man. He healed me. He set me free from the prison of my own body. *I* believe."

The more she spoke the stronger her words became, until the fervor of her statement rang across the water like the strike of a bell, and along with it came the words of Isaiah, which Tikva had heard time and time again from her father's lips. "I, the Lord, have called you in righteousness; I will take hold of your hand. I will keep you and will make you to be a covenant for the people and a light for the Gentiles, to open eyes that are blind, to free captives from prison and to release from the dungeon those who sit in darkness."

Tikva had always thought of the Messiah as the mighty king who would remove the shackles placed upon the Jews by the Romans and set them free, but could it be that even such a thing as leprosy, which had chained Na'ami in captivity, might also be broken by the One whom Adonai would send? She shook the thought from her mind, along with the reminder that she, too, felt imprisoned by her affliction.

"So how," asked Tikva, "if you could not get within any distance of this rabbi, did you come to be healed, Na'ami?"

A little grin curved the young woman's lips, and a light came into those green eyes that made them glitter like the surface of the sea. "*He* came to *me*."

"You see," interjected Chavah, obviously used to speaking for her daughter after so many years of dependence, "there are so many beggars here, all clamoring to see Yeshua for one reason or the other, that no one in Capernaum has a spare coin. And since we were determined to stay, we had to discover some way to live. As you can see"—she gestured to the lake before them that teemed with vessels, small and large—"fishing is an important way of life here and in all the little villages that line the beaches. So Hiram and Levon decided to try their hand at finding work with one of the teams. But no one had any room for them."

"We almost gave up," said Hiram. "Our bellies were snarling something fierce, but Levon had watched some of the men working on the boats and decided to make his own net, hoping we could at least wade out near the place a stream empties into the lake and catch a meal or two."

Chavah snorted, flashing a grin at Levon. "You should have seen his first attempt. Any fish would have been glad to get snared in such an easily escaped piece of netting. Holes as big as a man's head."

Hiram nodded, his gap-toothed mouth stretched wide with amusement as he prodded the silent man next to him. "That it was. But it was the thing that caught the attention of some of Yeshua's men."

"True," said Chavah. "Two of them noticed Levon, stripped to his waist, bobbing around in the water with his useless net and Hiram on the shore laughing at him. They offered their help. After the net was made secure and three fish lay on the beach, they asked how he came to be in Capernaum. Hiram told our tale, and about our mission to place Na'ami before Yeshua."

"At this point, we did not even know who the men were, nor their connection to the rabbi," said Hiram. "Just that they'd been knowledgeable and kind."

Chavah nodded, prodding the dying cook-fire with a stick. "They went their separate ways, without a hint that they knew the rabbi. It was not until the next morning that he came."

"He came to you, here on the beach?" asked Tikva.

"He did. We'd not seen him up close of course, so to us he was a stranger. But when he asked to speak to my daughter privately and asked for her by name—which neither Hiram nor Levon had told the men—we knew something was happening."

The hair on Tikva's neck prickled. Surely one of them must have spoken her name at some point. A mere man could not divine such things without help, could he?

"What did he say to you? How did he heal you?" Tikva asked Na'ami, her heart racing with anticipation.

The young woman's smile was wistful, her eyes full of secrets. "I can only say that we walked down the beach, not even out of sight of the others and talked together. He asked if I wanted to be healed, and I replied that there was nothing else I desired in the world. Then"—she turned to look directly in Tikva's eyes, her expression full of meaning—"he touched my face."

The significance of the moment was not lost on Tikva. It was considered unseemly for a man to touch a woman who was not his wife or close relation. And indeed many men, like her own father, did not even speak to strange women. And this man was considered a rabbi. A holy man. A man who would, after touching a leprous woman, be declared unclean himself.

And yet knowing all these things, he'd lowered himself to touch Na'ami, who likely had not been touched by any other hand than her mother's for years and years.

Tikva's throat was coated with fire, and tears pressed at the backs of her eyes. As she'd sensed from the first time she'd met Na'ami, there was no one else she'd ever known who could truly understand what it was like to be zavah for twelve years. To be an outcast. To be despised for something she had no control over. To be hidden away and deemed untouchable. And yet Yeshua had touched this woman without hesitation.

"Then what happened?" Simcha asked, as if sensing that Tikva was unable to speak.

"He told me to go out there"—she gestured to the body of water in front of them—"and submerse myself. I obeyed, of course, although I was confused."

Immediately, the story of Naaman, the Aramean commander who'd been healed of leprosy by the prophet Elisha, sprang to Tikva's mind. He had been told to dip his body in the Jordan, and that very same river fed the lake by which they stood.

"I cannot describe the moment I was healed. It is far beyond words," she said, those secrets flitting around in her green eyes again. "But when I came out of the water, dripping and shivering, I unwound the linen bandages from my hands. There was no more scaly and tough skin, no more weeping lesions, and no more pain. It was just smooth and clear and pink, as if I'd scrubbed my entire body with sand—although I'd done nothing of the sort." The secrets in her eyes had been replaced with awe. "I was, in a word, *free*."

"Did he then ask you for payment of some sort?"

"No." Na'ami's brows furrowed. "He was gone by the time I emerged from the water, back to wherever he'd come from, I assume. But he did not ask for money. The only thing he asked me for…" She halted, a gentle smile on her lips as she gazed out toward the water that had washed her clean.

Of course. There had to be something the man had demanded. No matter how holy he was considered, there was a price to everything, as Tikva was only too aware.

"He asked me to tell no one what we'd spoken of."

Tikva blinked in confusion.

"And so, although I can tell you that yes, we spoke, and yes, he healed me," Na'ami said, as she lifted two leprosy-free fingers to her rose-colored lips and then placed them in the center of her chest, "the rest will stay hidden in my heart, for the entirety of my days."

CHAPTER SEVENTEEN

❖

After Simcha and Tikva had taken leave of Na'ami and the rest of their group, with promises to find them again soon, the two made their way back up the narrow path and away from the water's edge.

"What do you think of all they had to say?" asked Simcha, using his crutch to press back a branch that blocked their way.

"There is much to ponder," said Tikva. "But I also know what I saw. Na'ami *was* afflicted with leprosy. She drew back her veils to show me the morning I met the four of them. I saw the lesions. It looked so awful, Simcha, so painful. But now… If I had not recognized her uniquely colored eyes I would not have known her. Truly, it is a miracle."

"Then you do believe that this Yeshua is a true healer? Even after all you've endured at the hands of those who claim the same?" he asked.

Tikva flushed, wondering just how much Helena had told him of the many humiliating and futile treatments all those midwives, physicians, and charlatans had subjected her to. A vision of Damianos and the horrors within his home rose up in her mind.

"I do not know anything for sure. But this I can say: Nothing of what Na'ami described was anything like my own experiences.

The men and women who insisted their methods could cure me demanded money every time, in advance of course. I suspect that much of the reason Helena was forced to sell her home within the first year of her husband's death was due to the extravagant fees of such people." This was something that Tikva felt no small amount of guilt over, but anytime she'd tried to bring up the conversation with Helena, her mother-in-law refused to discuss the past.

"And you?" she asked. "What do you think of all of this?"

Simcha was silent for a few moments, his gaze on the rocky path ahead.

"I believe you when you say that Na'ami was afflicted. And I believe that somehow this man healed her. But the claims that he could be the Messiah are what concern me. This is no small thing. If he were to lay claim to the throne of David—and of course, I know nothing of his lineage—not only would Herod Antipas have something to say of it, but even Rome might be stirred by such an extraordinary announcement. We've suffered the effects of failed rebellion before and the problems the Zealots have provoked with their attacks on those whom they consider collaborators with Rome."

"Do you think this Yeshua is a Zealot? Or that he is planning some sort of action against our leaders?"

"There is no way to know," said Simcha. "But after hearing what Na'ami has to say, I am determined to see you brought before him, claimant to the throne or not."

Tikva halted. "Why, Simcha? Why have you come here with me? Why leave your daughter and your business to help me find a healer, especially when the chances are so slim that I may even come within a few paces of him?"

Turning to face her, Simcha's eyes traveled over her face, likely taking in the paleness of her skin and the way it was drawn tight over her fragile bones like some ancient crone. He was a good man, a kind and generous one. Perhaps it was merely pity that drove him.

"The four of them are beggars, am I correct?" asked Simcha, throwing her line of thought into disarray.

"Yes," she admitted. "The cart lost its wheel on the road one morning as I took pottery to the market. No one else would stop to help me. I thought I might have to wait for hours until you discovered that I was missing and searched me out. But they stopped. Hiram and Levon fixed the wheel and Chavah told me of their desire to find Yeshua for Na'ami's sake. I know they aren't people with whom others might associate, especially when Na'ami was unclean and with Chavah's past as a woman of ill-repute—"

Simcha broke into her explanation. "Do you not know me at all, Tikva? When have I ever made a distinction between rich and poor, clean or unclean, acceptable or not?" He gestured to his foot. "I grew up on the outside too."

Embarrassment swept through her. "Of course not. I meant no offense. But you must remember that I grew up on the opposite side of those fences. My father is a Pharisee. Those distinctions were ingrained in me from the time I was a little girl. It was a shock to be thrown over that partition, alone. And it was not until I met Chavah and her group that I began to realize that even after twelve years of being shunned by the family that was supposed to love me without condition, I was still subscribing to my father's arrogant attitudes."

Anger pinched Simcha's dark brows. "I have never understood how your family could do such a thing to you, just toss you aside as if you were refuse. I'd hoped that when you first became ill they would take you in and give you sanctuary. I stayed away, only hearing rumors from people in the market, but then I heard that they refused to see you. That your father had declared you unfit to cross his threshold…" His jaw worked back and forth, fury flattening his lips into a thin line. "It was all I could do to not knock on his door and declare him a coward."

Tikva was shocked at the vehemence from Simcha's mouth, something she'd rarely heard before from the soft-spoken man.

"Once I'd tempered my first reaction, I decided the better thing would be to offer my assistance to you. Well…of course I did offer more than that." A blush ruddied his cheeks. "But I understood why you did not want to take me as a husband and was glad that you at least took up my offer of partnership."

Tikva felt a tremor beneath her breastbone as she considered speaking things aloud that she'd never before had the courage to say. But somehow, after hearing Na'ami tell of her healing, she'd finally allowed a tiny seed of hope to take root, and small buds of promise had already begun pressing above the surface.

"I never considered you unworthy to take as a husband, Simcha. I hope you know that. If circumstances in my life were different, if I was not…" Her own blush seared her cheeks, and she dropped her gaze to her sandals to avoid his eyes. "If I was not perpetually zavah, and was able to be who you needed me to be, then I would have been proud to be your wife." Her words had drifted into a near whisper.

His response was threaded with tight emotion. "And what if Yeshua does heal you, Tikva? What then? Will you be my wife?"

A huff of surprise slipped from her lips. "You still want such a thing?"

"Of course," he said, his tone strident.

"But…" She gestured to her face. "I have withered away into nothing. I look haggard, as if some foul spirit has sucked the life and youth from my bones."

"Your beauty has never been in question, Tikva. I thought you lovely as a young girl, with your sweet laughter teasing my thirsty ears. I thought you lovely that awful day you stood before me at my pottery stall and admired my work before you collapsed to the ground, and I have thought you more lovely every day since, whether you are treading clay, pushing a rickety cart back and forth like a pack mule to keep my business from folding in on itself, or adoring my Adina and giving her as much selfless love as any mother."

Simcha stepped closer then and for the first time slipped his hand into hers. "I will never push you to accept my offer, Tikva. But even though my initial proposal to you was one of a desperate man to a woman in need, this one is from a man whose respect and care for you has only deepened over the last twelve years. No matter whether Yeshua heals you or not, I still want you to be my wife. A joining in spirit and purpose, if not in body. Adina sees you as her mother, and I see you as a partner in all things."

Shock had flooded Tikva's limbs, making it nearly impossible to take another step. Things that had seemed to be so unattainable, so unfathomable even a few days ago were suddenly real possibilities in the wake of these revelations about Yeshua. She'd need time however, to weigh her feelings on the matter.

"And what of you?" she asked, hoping to delay responding to his proposal for now. "Do you desire healing as well?"

Simcha's expectant expression melted into sobriety. "I don't think it's even possible. I was born this way. It was not an illness developed later in life like you and Na'ami."

"Surely a man who can raise someone from the dead and cleanse a leper of her spots could see to your hand and foot as well, whether inborn or not. Chavah speaks of blind men given sight and the lame walking again. Surely some of those people were born with such afflictions."

He splayed the fingers on his deformed hand wide, glaring down at the two stubs as if in rebuke and then with an air of contemplation. "I wonder how it might be if he did. Would my fingers regrow themselves? Like the tail of a lizard? Or would they simply appear brand-new, my wrist straight and limber?"

He tapped his crutch against his clubbed foot, which, being too misshapen for normal footwear, was always wrapped in a few layers of protective cloth. A mischievous grin tipped one side of his mouth, and his brown eyes glittered. "One thing is for sure. I'd have to purchase a second sandal."

CHAPTER EIGHTEEN

❖

It had been three days since Yeshua and his men left this side of the Kinneret, three days since the horrific storm blew through, and three days of nervous anticipation for Tikva. Still disheartened by the news that sometimes the healer traveled throughout the countryside for weeks, she feared that Meira and her company might leave before she even had the chance to come before him. But with Na'ami's clear skin as witness of the miraculous, she allowed herself to pray that if Adonai willed it, somehow she would be afforded the opportunity.

Na'ami had said nothing more about her encounter with the rabbi on the beach that day, but the glow of health that surrounded the girl was only matched by the luminescence of her countenance. There was nothing left of the downtrodden, hurting woman Tikva had met in Ptolemais. It was as if Yeshua had not only healed her body, but her soul.

Although she tried not to, Tikva could not help but feel jealous of the transformation. Yes, she'd been given new hope by Na'ami's healing, but twelve years of grief and pain could not be washed away in a moment, even if the bleeding were to cease. She still had no family, for she was certain that even were she no longer zavah her father still would count her as dead to him. She'd still lost her husband, her baby, and everything she'd ever owned. She no longer had even a single mite to her name after Damianos had taken the last of it. And of course, her youth and its bright promises could never be reclaimed.

Although she was still reeling from Simcha's renewed proposal of marriage, she'd said nothing to Meira, Na'ami, and Chavah, with whom she'd come to the market this morning. The three of them had become acquainted in the courtyard of the potter's house when Na'ami and Chavah sought Tikva out the day before. The women had been eager to tell Tikva of another witness to Yeshua's miracles, this one a woman whose legs had been withered and useless and who now walked unimpeded. Simcha's afflictions came to mind immediately, and her conviction that both of them must somehow win an audience with Yeshua solidified at this news.

The four women had carried baskets of fish to the market just after dawn, the fruit of Levon's and Hiram's nighttime labors now that they'd found employment on a fishing vessel out of Tabgha. Springs of warm water emptied into the lake near the tiny village just south of Capernaum, drawing an abundance of fish, along with the Galileans who made their living catching them.

Not only had Yeshua's men taught them how to weave superior nets, apparently they'd also recommended Levon and Hiram to one of their acquaintances. Both men were delighted over the prospect of steady work and felt that this gift far outweighed any healing of their own bodies that Yeshua might have offered.

One thing was clear. The four of them were beggars no more, as evidenced by the four heavy baskets that sat at the feet of Tikva and the other women in the market, the coins that now jingled in the purse Chavah carried around her neck, and her once-empty sack that was now fairly bursting with bartered grain.

With the proceeds, Chavah had already purchased a measure of salt from another vendor. She'd also offered Meira and Tikva a portion of the profits if they'd be willing to help her and her daughter prepare the unsold fish to dry in the sun, ensuring that none of Levon and Hiram's portion of the night's catch would be wasted.

Now that their stock was over halfway depleted and the sunlight had strengthened, the women had decided to return to the beach and begin the gruesome but necessary task of gutting the leftovers so they could be salted and laid out on racks before they began to ripen.

"I will carry this one," said Meira, hoisting one of the baskets to her hip. "Na'ami, can you carry the other?"

"We can split the remainder between the four baskets, so the burden is equal," said Tikva.

"No," said Meira, a pinch between her dark brows as she surveyed Tikva's face. "You look exhausted, my friend. Even more pale than usual. I won't have you faint in this heat. Chavah can manage the grain sack."

Although pricked with guilt that she was so useless, Tikva felt gratitude flood her heart. After so many years of solitude, with only her mother-in-law and a little girl for female company, she felt that even these new friendships were a miracle in themselves. A former prostitute, a leper, and a Phoenician treated her with more kindness than all the friends she'd had since childhood.

The women made their way back through the crowd, headed toward the place Chavah and her group had been encamped near the water. But just as they entered the main square, the doors of the synagogue burst open, and a horde of men poured out of the building, blocking their way. Most of them were dressed in the distinctive robes of the Pharisee, with the customary phylacteries on their arms and foreheads. A meeting of rabbis, Tikva guessed, or perhaps a gathering of the town's Sanhedrin.

A cacophony of angry voices filled the air as the swarm of bodies swirled about the square. Whatever these men had been discussing within the synagogue had spilled into the street with them.

"He is nothing of the sort!" cried out one of the men.

"You have no evidence to the contrary!" snapped another.

"Should we turn back and try another route?" asked Meira, hefting the basket higher on her hip.

Frowning, Chavah gestured toward the crowd that had gathered behind them now as well. It seemed that the loud argument had drawn an audience from the commoners in the streets. "They'll disperse shortly," she said. "We had best wait, or we'll be trampled. I don't want Tikva to be knocked about."

Tikva had been witness to more than a few heated discussions between rabbis outside the synagogue in Ptolemais, especially when one of the rich and powerful Sadducees was involved. In fact, many such loud disputes had been waged in her own home among her father's friends and rivals. But the vehemence with which these men were debating shocked her.

Uneasiness made Tikva pull her veil tight across her face and shift closer to Na'ami. Not only would these men view her presence here as an abomination if they knew what she was, but the red faces and raised fists of the most vocal participants made her fear that they might resort to violence to solve this disagreement.

"He is nothing but a pretender," said a man about three paces from Tikva.

"And what of the miracles here in this very town?" shot back another. "I was there when he caused a blind man to see. And we all saw the changes in Baruch after the demons were cast out of him. And the way that centurion's slave was rescued from certain death. Only Adonai could grant such power."

A loud chorus of shouts went up at this testimony, many decrying his witness as lies and some asking for the man to be heard. Realizing at once that this fight was over the very man she'd come to Capernaum to see, all thoughts of escaping this assembly fled Tikva's mind, and she tilted forward on her toes to peer at the leaders who stood on the porch of the synagogue. Their dark robes flapped in a breeze that had mercifully just swept in off the water to stir the stagnant air. Most of their expressions were full of thunder as they gazed out over the roiling, shouting crowd, but two of them stood off to the side, with something more like curiosity on their faces as they listened to the discussion, as if not as firm in their convictions about Yeshua as many of the others.

"You call this man rabbi? Who is his teacher?" retorted a Pharisee not far from Tikva. "He is certainly not one of our number. Under whose authority does he speak?"

"None!" cried out a few voices.

"He is nothing more than a carpenter from Nazareth," yelled someone. "The only authority he has is over sticks and stones!"

Derisive laughter went up around them.

One of the men who did not wear the robes of a Pharisee spoke up. "There are plenty of witnesses, some right here in Capernaum, who can testify to the healings that have taken place. Let us bring some of them, along with their families, here before the council."

"None would be a reliable witness. They are likely paid to spread lies," sneered one of the rabbis on the porch. "This Sanhedrin will not sully itself by entertaining such a farce. This man should be driven from our town. Perhaps even from Galilee. Send him to Jerusalem. The priests can deal with him there. Let them bring him to heel."

"He is gathering too much of a following," agreed the Pharisee next to him. "The Romans will take notice. We don't need them sniffing around our town."

A murmur of agreement went up around the square. Indeed, although Capernaum was ultimately governed by Rome and its appointed rulers, like Ptolemais, the local Sanhedrin was granted authority in civil and religious matters, as long as they understood that authority was granted by Caesar and his underlings. If even a whiff of rebellion were to float before the nostrils of Rome, Capernaum would be punished, and the town Sanhedrin's powers stripped.

"'Let us return to the Lord,'" quoted one man whose face Tikva could not see, speaking the words of the prophet Hosea in a deep, rich voice from the center of the group. "'He has torn us to pieces but he will heal us.'"

A brief pause ensued, as if the entire crowd was collectively holding its breath, before chaos erupted. Tikva and her companions exchanged horrified glances, pressing in closer to one another.

"You dare to equate this charlatan with the Almighty?" screamed one of the Pharisees from the porch of the synagogue, whose ostentatious phylactery spanned from his hairline to his brows. "Such words are an affront to all we hold sacred."

"This Yeshua is telling the people to disregard the Torah!" yelled one man, fist raised. "A false prophet must be put to death for inciting rebellion against Adonai. Moses says we must purge the evil from among us."

Loud affirmations went up around the square. But one of the men on the porch lifted his palms, as if to restore order to the rage brewing before him.

"That is a serious accusation," said the Pharisee, whom Tikva guessed might be the leader of the assembly by his air of authority and the height of his decorative turban. "Do you have specific testimony of his speaking against the Law of Moses?"

A rumble of chatter grew around the square but none present raised their voices to give such an account.

"There is no need to stir his followers into a frenzy," said the leader, his tone placating and surprisingly calm. "These ridiculous claims of healings will prove themselves to be false, and he will fade into obscurity. Of this I have no doubt."

But the healings are *true,* thought Tikva. *I am standing here beside a woman who could give testimony to such.* She glanced over at Na'ami, whose lips were pressed together in a straight line. She likely was incensed by the accusations and wished she could march up to the porch and lay out her own case. But Tikva knew she would not. Very few Pharisees accepted a woman's word as legitimate testimony. And a beggar's, even less so. Besides, if she refused to tell even her mother all that transpired with Yeshua, what hope was there that she would open her mouth before an assembly of furious men?

"He is the Messiah!" shouted someone from among the common crowd at Tikva's back. "He has come to save us!"

Another roar of disapproval went up from among the learned men.

With a scowl, the head Pharisee raised his palms, a silent demand for order. As if they were simply children sitting at the feet of their father, the men quieted with surprising ease.

"You say this man is our Messiah?" asked the leader, brows lifted in mocking. "What proof have you? We've already established that these so-called healings are likely nothing but rumor and myth."

He waited as the crowd shuffled and murmured.

"You mean to tell me"—he spread his arms wide, his voice strengthening with each word—"that a carpenter from

Nazareth, who wanders Galilee with a motley group of fishermen and tax collectors, prostitutes and beggars, is the King we've been waiting for? This man who is rumored to have been born to an unwed girl is the inheritor to the throne of David?" He waited, scanning the crowd for anyone brave enough to answer the question.

"If so, then where is his army?" he continued. "If this Yeshua is the one who will break the chains of our oppressors, how will he overcome the might of Caesar? Will he and his blind and lame flock march on Rome?"

This statement garnered a laugh from the Pharisees.

"Will they raise Israel back to its birthright by using their crutches as swords and their unclean bandages as slings? We all know the prophecies of the Messiah. We teach them to you here." He gestured to the synagogue behind him. "And none of them points to some obscure woodworker as the mighty savior and rescuer of our nation. Or is there some passage I have neglected to study? Is it in the Teaching of Moses? Or the Prophets? Perhaps the Writings? Or maybe among the words of the ancient rabbis who've come before us? Show me, and I will believe such nonsense too." His raised his palms, entreating the assembly to rise to the challenge.

"No?" The leader smiled indulgently when no one spoke, confident in his extensive education in the Torah, both written and oral. "As I said before, this man is nothing more than a liar, a charlatan, and, if proven to be speaking against Moses and the Torah, a lawbreaker. Best to let this fervor die its own natural death. Either the Romans tire of his antics and throw him in prison or the truth catches up with him and his followers disband." He waved a hand in the air, as if the whole situation was nothing but a minor annoyance to be batted away. "One way or the other, he'll disappear."

The lead Pharisee's speech seemed to have soothed some of the anger that had been threatening to explode earlier. The men who had come from the synagogue took to grouping themselves in threes and fours, discussing all that had been said.

"Come," said Chavah, grasping Tikva's arm. "We should be able to find our way through the crowd now. You look like a sheet of linen strung on a line."

Indeed, Tikva had found herself drained of energy by the tension in the square, along with the silent argument that had waged within her own mind as they'd debated. She may not be a learned man like they were, but she'd sat at the feet of her father, who, in spite of his attitudes toward women in public, had allowed her to silently listen in on the daily lessons he taught her brothers. She'd never read the words of the Torah from a scroll, but they'd been burned in her heart while listening to her father's voice recite them day after day for as long as she could remember.

Was there something in the Torah that pointed to Yeshua as Messiah? Or were the leaders of the synagogue correct that the man who would sit on David's throne would be the very embodiment of the exalted warrior-poet himself?

Lost in her musings, Tikva allowed Chavah to guide her through the crowd. They took care to not come in contact with any of the men but received more than a few glares for their audacity at cutting through the assembly. Although Chavah kept her chin high, seemingly unfazed by the status of the men surrounding her, Tikva kept her eyes on the ground, concentrating on each step and praying they would escape the square without further notice.

"I want to hear this man for myself," said one of the Pharisees as they passed. "I did not come all the way from Ptolemais to accept the word of others."

Shock caused Tikva's feet to halt, which pulled Chavah to a stop as well. The man was from her own town? If he was, he would undoubtedly know her father. Taking care to pull her veil tight over her face to obscure her features, Tikva turned around slowly, taking inventory of the three men who stood in a group behind her.

"I agree," said another in the group, his voice lowered and his eyes flitting toward the synagogue steps, as if the leaders there might hear him. "There are too many rumors floating around about this in our own congregation. But if the three of us return with firm witness that this man is a fraud, we can quash this nonsense once and for all."

Tikva gulped down a wayward cry as she took in the faces of the group and then spun to ward off any chance that they might recognize her. Not only was the first man known to her, one she'd dined with on more than a few occasions at her father's house, but the other two looked vaguely familiar as well. All three of them were most definitely from her hometown. And she, of course, was the infamous Unclean Woman of

Ptolemais. These men could proclaim her a known zavah in the hearing of this gathering of consecrated men, and she could very well be arrested for willfully coming into contact with them and thereby making them unclean as well.

Flushed with false energy that she knew would abandon her shortly, and with her heart pounding so loudly she thought it alone might cause her father's acquaintances to notice her, she pressed on toward the southern edge of the square, her three friends now in *her* wake.

By the time Tikva had burst free of the crowd, legs shaking and palms and back sweating, she'd decided that whether or not Yeshua was the Messiah, she would still go to him. Frankly, it mattered little to her if he was some future King of Israel. She only wanted to be set free from this present prison of her broken body and the shame that accompanied it. She could only pray that he would return before someone recognized her and stripped her of the last of the filthy tatters that remained of her dignity.

CHAPTER NINETEEN

"He has returned! He has returned!"

The voice of a young boy running down the street near the potter's house caused a stir among the traders who'd been encamped within his front courtyard for the past four nights.

Zuri, the closest to the gate, ran out into the alley and snagged the child by the tunic before he could run away.

"Who has returned? Why are you shouting?" he asked the squirming boy.

"Let me go!" The boy pushed at Zuri for a moment but then seemed to decide his best chance to escape the enormous Phoenician's grip was to answer the question. "Yeshua. Yeshua has returned from across the water. His boat landed only a few moments ago. Let me go." He struggled again. "I was told to announce his arrival."

Zuri glanced over at Tikva, a smile curling on his lips. "Where? Where is he now?"

The boy shrugged. "South near Tabgha. Wherever he is there's always a crowd. It's never hard to find him."

Zuri freed the child, who continued on, his exuberant announcement ringing off the walls of the mud-brick homes all along the alleyway.

Stunned by the thought that today was finally the day she might come before the healer, Tikva did not hear Simcha's approach.

"Come," he said, his calm voice doing battle against the chaos that was building inside her head. "It is time."

She blinked up at the man who'd accompanied her across the country at the expense of his own business, who'd entrusted her with his daughter even though she'd refused to be his wife, whose warm brown eyes looked on her with what she now realized was more than just simple kindness, and found a deep sense of comfort in his presence.

"Yes," she said, meeting his gaze with an expression that she hoped made him understand that she was not just agreeing with his gentle command but with the question that he'd asked on the beach.

His smile, and the deep grooves around his wide mouth that proved his genuine and joyful nature, lit a new spark in her heart. She'd thought him handsome before now, but in this moment, she found him breathtaking.

"Yes?" he echoed, a hint of awe in his voice.

She returned his smile. If this man was willing to marry her whether her body was healed by Yeshua or not, then why wouldn't she accept him? Who would be foolish enough to turn away a man who'd given her so much over the last twelve years without asking for a thing in return? Even if her body only afforded her a few more months of life, she'd want to spend it by his side. But perhaps, if Adonai willed it, they might marry with bodies made miraculously whole.

"Then let's go find Yeshua," he said, with a tug to her elbow.

"We will come with you," said Zuri, his arm about his wife's waist. "I've heard plenty about this carpenter rabbi. I'd like to see him for myself."

Meira asked one of the other women among their group to search out Na'ami and Chavah on the beach and let them know that they'd gone to find Yeshua, but Tikva suspected that they would already have known why she and Meira would not join their fish-drying efforts this afternoon.

Twelve years ago, almost to this very day, she'd stood on the bluff watching for her Asa to come home, a baby in her belly and hope in her heart. Would this be the day that all the shame and pain she'd endured since that time finally ceased? She kept the image of Na'ami's bright and clear visage in her mind as she followed Simcha from the courtyard, down the alley, and toward Capernaum, and she prayed that it would be the last stretch of road both she and Simcha endured with broken bodies.

◆

She'd heard about the crowds that followed Yeshua around the countryside, but this teeming mass of humanity gathered in a rocky field near Tabgha was shocking. Where had they all been? Hiding in the caves up on the mountain that stood above the Kinneret? Sleeping out in the wilderness? Or had they been absorbed into the many villages that lined the lakeshore? Wherever they'd been, somehow they'd heard of his return and had gathered here with the very same purpose as Tikva and Simcha.

Between the loud supplications to the man whom no one could even see from this distance, the squawks and shrieks of children who'd joined their parents to watch the spectacle, and the roiling chatter among the multitude, Tikva's ears rang with the clamor.

"How will we ever get through?" she asked Simcha, whose mouth no longer wore the elation from her earlier acceptance of his proposal.

His brown eyes traveled over the crowd, his expression troubled. "I don't know. It seems impossible," he said, but then an expression of pure determination settled on the planes of his face, one she recognized from times at the pottery wheel when the clay was not cooperating with his ministrations. "But I won't stop until you are in front of him."

"Nor will I," said Zuri, as he moved in front of them, using his bulk to press between bodies. Meira held to the back of her husband's tunic, and in turn, Tikva grasped hers. Simcha kept to the rear of their little caravan, making apologies for Zuri, and sometimes his own wayward crutch, as he hobbled along behind.

They'd not even made it to the center of the crowd when word rolled back through the mass that the rabbi was going to speak. An expectant hush settled over the crowd, and most of the group suddenly sat down in their places, affording Tikva her first view of the man she'd traveled so far to entreat.

Although there were a number of men standing in his vicinity, most of them waving at the crowd in an obvious command for the multitude to settle on the ground, it was plain to Tikva who their leader was. Standing at their center, Yeshua waited, his arms folded over his chest and his body as still as one of the pillars in the synagogue.

She could not distinguish his features from so far away, but from what she could see he looked no different than most of the men with whom she was acquainted. However, there was something in his stance, something that suggested unbending authority as he waited for the crowd to settle. His very stillness and the steady gaze he directed toward the people did more to calm them than his gesticulating men, and soon only a few crying babies broke the quiet.

Then, he began to speak.

She could not hear his words—they were swallowed up by the rustle of the breeze in the trees that lined both sides of the empty field in which they'd gathered. And even those repeated in whispers among the people came to her ears as broken thoughts and disjointed stories, nothing of true significance. Every bone in her body yearned to jump up and run to the front of this assembly, to hear with her own ears what poured from the mouth of this carpenter-turned-rabbi.

Frustration welled as the people around her began to grow restless, and the afternoon waned. This was not how she'd envisioned this encounter with Yeshua. In her mind, she and Simcha had walked right to him, respectfully asked for his healing and then, like Na'ami, had found their bodies whole.

How foolish and naive she'd been to think that these last few steps to freedom would not be difficult!

"Did you hear what happened during the storm?" asked one of the women sitting in front of Tikva to her companion.

Her friend shook her head. "I arrived only this morning from near Beit She'an. I've come to plead with the rabbi to heal my boy." She shifted a sleeping child of about three years on her lap, brushing his disheveled hair from his forehead. The boy's lip was misshapen, curling nearly up to his nose, a large gap where his front teeth should be. She wiped a line of saliva from his chin and pressed a kiss to his cheek.

"I heard the story from my husband, who is a friend of Shimon. They've fished these same waters for many years." She gestured to one of Yeshua's companions standing off to the side, his eyes trained on his leader. "He said that as soon as they left this side of the water, a storm kicked up without warning, right over their vessel."

As she had when the wine merchant spoke of the same incident, Tikva remembered well how the clouds had swirled over the Kinneret that evening, brewing and roiling with inordinate strength as she and the other traders huddled beneath wagons and in their makeshift tents.

"Shimon told my husband that Yeshua was exhausted that evening and had already fallen asleep in the hull. Although the sound of the wind was like a hundred roaring lions, and the waves tossed the boat about like a piece of driftwood, he remained asleep."

"How did they survive such a thing?" asked the woman.

"I don't know. More than a few vessels have met the lake bed during one of those gales. And many fisherman have met their fate there."

Much like my own husband, thought Tikva with a sharp pang of latent grief for Asa, whose own bones rested on the seafloor.

The fisherman's wife gestured to the lake that stretched across their field of view, its waters gleaming golden as the sun began to sink at their backs. "But what I do know," she said, "is that when his men finally succeeded in waking him, he stood up, lifted his arms wide, and told the wind and waves to be still."

The woman laughed, causing her sleeping child to squirm in his sleep. She rocked him back and forth until he quieted again.

"I laughed at such an idea as well," said the fisherman's wife. "But, since you are not from here, you would not remember how all of a sudden, seemingly at the height of its power, the storm simply ceased. None of us in Capernaum had ever seen such a thing. We'd been huddled in our homes as the wind lashed at the shutters, and palm branches and tree limbs flew through the air and then, just…nothing."

Tikva noticed a few others in the area nodding in agreement.

"Shimon told my husband that within moments of Yeshua's words, the wind stopped and the waves melted away. The water became like glass all around them. And when they looked up at the sky that had been practically green in its fury, the stars above them were clear and bright."

Tikva's father's voice was suddenly in her mind, as clear and bright as those stars had been as he spoke the words of the psalmist from ancient times. *"Then they cried out to the Lord in their trouble, and he brought them out of their distress. He stilled the storm to a whisper; the waves of the sea were hushed."*

The leader of the synagogue had been adamant that nowhere within the *Tanakh* were there allusions that Yeshua might be the Messiah. But, if this story was true, and he had indeed calmed the storm the other night with only his words…

Was the man standing perhaps only a hundred paces before her the one who would sit on the throne of David? Had he come to rescue her people from their enslavement to Rome and to raise Israel back to its prominence among the nations?

A stirring excitement brewed in her chest. Were rabbis wrong about how the Messianic age came about? Could a carpenter from Nazareth, as obscure a place as any other little village, one day use the enemies of Israel as a footstool just as Adonai, through David, had promised?

The head Pharisee's jest about the lame and the blind rising as his army warred against this new revelation, but surely a man who had power over the water and the sky could defeat Caesar, couldn't he?

So many questions layered one atop the other in her heart, deafening her ears to anything else the two women or anyone else around her said, that Tikva barely noticed when the people in front of them began standing.

By the time she realized that the crowd was shifting, some of them shaking their heads as they walked away, Simcha had made his way to his feet and was offering her a hand to stand as well.

"What is happening?" she asked, as she brushed the dust from her tunic.

Simcha frowned. "The sun will be going down soon. The crowd has been told to disperse for the day."

Tears flooded her eyes as she grabbed his wrist to halt him before he, too, walked away. "But…we haven't been given a chance to go before him." Standing on her toes, her gaze swept over the multitude toward the place Yeshua and his men had been standing. Only one or two remained, and their leader was nowhere to be seen.

"Where did he go?" she pleaded, her knees wavering as a wave of exhaustion hit her. Her body seemed to have been subsisting solely on hope since the boy's cry back at the potter's house, and without that hope, she felt like folding in on herself.

"He's likely been led to the home of one of his men," said Simcha.

"But we can't leave. What if he comes back?" She looked to Zuri and Meira for support, her fingers digging into Simcha's skin. "We must stay close by. Please, this is my only chance."

The couple exchanged sympathetic glances with Simcha, a wordless conversation seeming to go on in front of her.

"All right," said Simcha, his gaze skimming the remaining crowd, some of whom were already laying out mantles and blankets, obviously preparing to stay the night here in the field. "We will stay."

"We'll return to the potter's house," said Meira, "and bring you more food in the morning." Prepared as usual, Tikva's practical friend reached into the pack at her hip and handed them two dried fish and a handful of olives wrapped in a cut of linen.

"There looks to be a stream just there to the south," said Zuri, pointing toward the place a large group of people was gathered. "And it's plenty warm enough that you'll not need a fire tonight."

Meira unwound her outer garment from her body and wrapped it around Tikva's shoulders. "Try to stay in this same place so we can find you easily tomorrow, but if somehow that doesn't happen, we'll meet you back at the potter's home."

"Thank you," said Tikva, pulling the woolen wrap about her body. "You both have been so kind to us. Anyone who would allow strangers to tag along on their caravan, especially ones who are not able to carry the same load and have kept you here for three days longer than you meant to…"

Meira hushed her with a finger to her lips. "You are not strangers anymore. And it was our delight to bring you with us." She gazed toward the edge of the water. "And I pray that your God, or whoever else might have the power to direct such things, will bring you before that man. If even half the stories I've heard are true, then neither I nor Zuri will make one step back toward Ptolemais until he grants you audience."

After the couple parted from Tikva and Simcha, the two of them made their way over to the stream and, like pups, drank from its refreshing waters on their knees. Then, returning near to the place Zuri and Meira had left them, they settled on the ground as dusk rose over the far horizon.

Both she and Simcha seemed to be lost in their own thoughts, saying nothing as the light of a few fires burst into brilliance among the groups gathered throughout the field and the first stars twinkled into existence over the hills in the east. The smell of roasting fish made Tikva's stomach rumble, so she unwrapped the parcel Meira had handed her and divided the fish and the olives between the two of them.

"Get some sleep," said Simcha, when they'd finished their paltry meal. "Dawn will come sooner than we know, and you look far beyond exhausted."

Conceding that he was correct and that she was barely able to remain seated, Tikva rolled Meira's cloak into a long pillow, one that would accommodate both of them. Then she laid down and gestured for him to do the same. Any other time the two of them sleeping beside one another might be considered unseemly, but as weary as she was, she did not care. Besides, there was nothing hidden here when they were surrounded by hundreds of others in this field, and no one to question whether they were as yet unmarried.

Without protest, Simcha laid his head on the makeshift pillow, leaving an arms-length between them, his eyes on the stars that had now taken over the heavens.

"Did you mean what you said?" he asked. "Earlier in the courtyard?"

"I did," she replied.

"I am glad," he said, and she heard the smile in his voice. "Adina will be beside herself. She's been pleading with me to force you into marriage for months now."

She laughed, thinking of the lively girl with a will of iron. "That does not surprise me at all."

"She loves you," he said.

"And I her, as if she were my own." Her throat swelled as she laid her palm on her stomach, allowing herself to remember the sensation of her baby moving within her womb.

Reaching across the divide with his deformed hand, Simcha grasped hers. It did not matter that it was only three long fingers that wove between her own, only that his steadfast presence filled her with strength and comfort. She drifted to sleep, glad that no matter what happened tomorrow, she would soon lie next to him every night.

CHAPTER TWENTY

Tikva woke to the sight of dawn creeping over the horizon, gilding the hills in the far distance with a rose-hued glow, and the sound of a lark greeting the morning with song.

Turning over, she found that Simcha was still sleeping, his handsome face relaxed and boyish in the burgeoning light. The sight tempted her to brush the dark hair from his forehead and to stroke the beard that had not graced the cheeks of the boy who'd once watched her from afar so long ago. Resisting the instinct, she stood instead, feeling surprisingly refreshed after a night sleeping on the stony ground without even a blanket to cover her.

Once she'd found a secluded spot to tend her needs with a thick stand of trees nearby, she gazed over the water that stretched from one end of her vision to the other. She watched as three small vessels departed from the harbor down at Tabgha, heading out to begin their quest for the day's catch.

A sudden thought burst to life that made her heart stumble. Was Yeshua on one of those boats? Had he already left this shore to travel someplace else? Perhaps the crowd had been too overwhelming, and he needed to escape to somewhere he'd not be engulfed by supplicants, including her. Disappointment speared through her. Perhaps this entire journey had been in vain, and Simcha had wasted his time in accompanying her. How would she ever repay him if nothing came of all this effort? Would he be angry and decide he did not want to marry her after all?

Just when her hands began to shake as she contemplated how she would tell Helena and Adina that it all had been for naught, she caught sight of a figure down at the edge of the pebbled shoreline, on his knees. Although she was too far away to see anything more than his bent back and dark hair, something about him seemed familiar. Then, as the sun rose over the hills, his arms, and his face, lifted to the sky. It was Yeshua, of this she had no doubt. The same authority and calm that exuded from his person as he spoke yesterday now emanated from the still figure whose entire being seemed engaged in worship of the Creator, whose breath spoke the light itself into existence.

Awed and humbled by the thought, Tikva sank to her knees as well, blessings flowing from her lips to the One whose might had rescued her people from slavery to Pharaoh, whose faithfulness had sustained them throughout their sojourn in Babylon, and who promised that a Savior would arise to set them free once and for all. The idea that this very man might now be before her caused tears to flow freely down her cheeks. She bent farther to the ground, forehead pressed to the dirt, and let her prayers pour out in a mess of grief and dashed hopes and supplication to Adonai.

Just as she felt that every word of fear and doubt had been wrenched from her soul, the sounds of loud voices made her lift her head to search out the source.

"He's leaving!" a woman called out. "Heading into Capernaum!"

Sometime while she'd been praying, Simcha had awakened. He stood behind her now, rumpled and bleary-eyed as he balanced on his crutch.

"Come," he said, that piercing determination again in his expression. "We will follow wherever he goes."

A quiver of agreement pulsed against her ribs. If it took every last bit of strength within her ruined body, she would follow.

They joined the stream of bodies as they pushed toward the trade road that led into Capernaum. She must have been praying longer than she'd realized and missed his departure from the beach for him to already have made it halfway there.

Thankfully this early in the morning, the crowd was significantly smaller than yesterday. Through the fifty or so that walked in front of them six or seven abreast, she could even see some of his men, including the one the fisherman's wife had pointed out as Shimon. Excitement wrapped its welcome arms around her heart as Simcha urged her forward.

With a suddenness that caused her to stumble forward and run into the man in front of her, the entire procession came to a halt. The man turned to glare at her, his eyes traveling over her with disdain that made her all too aware that if anyone knew that she was, in fact, unclean, she'd have been dragged away, likely to the sound of cheers.

Stomach rolling, she mumbled an apology and pulled her head scarf farther down, knowing that in the eyes of most men a shrouded woman was invisible. She hoped they would not take another look.

"We have to get you closer," said Simcha directly into her ear. "Hold on to my tunic. I will push forward."

Somehow, he did just that. Perhaps it was that he was obviously a crippled man, or fear that his wooden crutch might mash a few toes, but the mass of bodies seemed to spread apart as he hobbled forward, although more than a few unkind words were said as they passed. Some commotion ahead of them seemed to be garnering most of the attention, however, so before she knew it, she and Simcha were within only a few paces of Yeshua and his men.

The reason for the halt became clear. Another crowd had met them on the road from Capernaum, blocking Yeshua's path and causing a flurry of confusion and frustration. Voices of distress lifted all around them.

Through the shifting and murmuring crowd, Tikva saw something that made her insides clench with worry. A group of three Pharisees stood off to one side of the road, and although their backs were to her, she could tell by their rigid stances that they were none too pleased with the scene in front of them. Had they come to challenge Yeshua? Or perhaps drag him off to be arrested like some of them had insisted was the best course of action in the square?

To her great surprise, one of their own stood in front of Yeshua, but his head was missing its distinctive turban, and his face was pale. Immediately she recognized him as one of the two Pharisees who'd stood on the porch of the synagogue with more curiosity than hostility on their faces.

"Please," he said, and the mass of people around her hushed expectantly, likely as surprised as she to hear a respected and honored leader of the synagogue plead with a man his leader had publicly declared a fraud.

"Please, my daughter is dying." His voice broke, and his knees buckled as he dropped to the ground, his head bowed. "She is my only child. I cannot bear to lose her. She is all I have left of my wife."

Tikva's heart went out to the man. She knew the pain he suffered. Losing her babe had been like losing Asa all over again.

"Please come to my home," begged the man. "Touch her. Heal her as you did the centurion's servant that day." He lifted his eyes to Yeshua. "I believe."

So do I, came the thought, unbidden, as if it were simply woven into the fabric of her soul.

Without a word, Yeshua reached down and lifted the man to his feet. Then, with His arm around the Pharisee, as if the two were the closest of friends, He began to walk beside him toward Capernaum.

The crowd swiftly closed in upon Simcha and Tikva as they moved forward, making it clear that it would be impossible to reach Yeshua now. He was headed toward the Pharisee's house, and by the time they arrived in Capernaum she and Simcha would be pushed to the very back of the crowd, since neither of them was able to keep up with ease.

She was so close and yet so very far away. A sob rose up in her throat.

The three Pharisees who had been off to the side of the road also moved to follow the crowd, and her pulse raced as she realized that they were the three men from Ptolemais who'd been so insistent on bringing proof of Yeshua's lies back to their congregation.

As if suddenly driven by a rush of renewed determination, Simcha ordered the people in front of him to move aside, to make way for him and his wife. To her horror, the sound of his voice encouraged the three men from her town to look toward them, and in the same moment she realized that in the commotion her head scarf had fallen away. Her face was uncovered before them.

Recognition flared in the eyes of her father's friend, and his face contorted into the most hideous expression of disgust. She felt the impact of the word before it even broke from his lips.

"Tameh! Tameh!" he called out, pointing at her through the crowd. "That woman is zavah! She is unclean."

The people around her began to mutter, asking whom he was speaking of.

"Go," said Simcha, the command breaking through the humiliation roiling through her body. "Get to Him. Don't stop until you do."

Then, without warning, he raised his crutch, swinging it wide and crying out, moving toward the shocked Pharisees as if he were possessed by some violent spirit.

The stunned crowd parted, giving him room to plow toward her accuser, and affording her the perfect path toward the Rabbi.

Although worried for Simcha, she obeyed his command, pushing forward through the last bodies that blocked her path toward the man she'd truly begun to believe was the Great Deliverer of her people, and who was the only one who could break her chains as well.

Again the voice of her father rose up in her mind, speaking the words of the Prophet Malachi.

"But for you who revere my name, the sun of righteousness will rise with healing in its rays."

If I can only touch Him, she thought, knowing that she would do nothing to prevent Him from reaching the Pharisee's daughter but desperate to be relieved of this burden she'd carried for so long. She kept her eyes pinned to the corner of His garment that flapped with blue knotted fringes at His side as He walked, like the fluttering of a bird taking flight into the morning.

With the last of her strength, she lunged, her bony fingers barely grazing Yeshua's tzitzit as she toppled forward into the dirt.

CHAPTER TWENTY-ONE

More than a few people must have passed her by as she knelt on the ground, but she barely noticed.

Something had changed.

Although her knees should be screaming in agony from the scrape of the stones under her skin, the only thing she could feel was the warm, delicious sensation inside her, as if a flame had burst to life deep in her abdomen. As blood rushed in her temples, blocking out the noise of the crowd around her, the feeling began to radiate from that one point into the rest of her body, flowing through her with the force of a mighty river. From the tips of her fingers to the soles of her feet, she was overwhelmed with tingling. Exhilarating joy swept over her as she realized that every bit of weariness had been washed away. Her limbs felt like feathers, as if she could take flight herself and wing into the sky. A laugh built in her chest as she named the feeling for what it was. Freedom. She'd been healed.

"Who touched me?" came a voice from nearby, breaking into her silent shouts of triumph.

Lifting her eyes, she peered around the legs of the people in front of her, who'd once again halted on the road. Sandals moved toward her.

"Who touched me?" the voice repeated.

A number of people around denied that it was them, and Tikva shuddered, knowing that it was she Yeshua was searching for. What would He do? With confusion in their voices, a few of His men insisted that there were too many people pressing in all around for them to determine who'd touched Him in the chaos.

Yeshua was not swayed by their argument. "Someone touched me, for I recognized power going out from me."

She'd not asked for this healing—perhaps He felt she'd stolen that power from Him. What was more, healed or not, she was still ritually unclean. And if Yeshua was a man consecrated for service to the Most High, then her touch, even if only to the wings of His garment, would have defiled Him. She pressed her lips tight, swallowing her gasp of fear, as the sandals came nearer. It was more than likely that He would turn and walk away when He realized who and what she was, those tzitzit whirling just like her father's had done outside the synagogue all those months ago. But there was nothing for her to do but take responsibility for what she had done.

"It was I," she called out. The crowd around her parted as she stood, trembling, and made her way toward Yeshua.

Unworthy to even look the man in the eye, she kept her head down as she knelt before Him, then placed her forehead in the dirt, upturned palms outstretched. The beautiful sensation of wholeness pulsed through her, giving her the courage to open her mouth.

"I am the one who touched You, my Lord. I have been zavah for twelve years."

She heard a few horrified gasps behind her. There were many people on this road whom she might have inadvertently touched today, not just Yeshua.

"From the day my baby was torn from my womb, I have bled. But the very moment I touched the fringe of Your garment, I was healed." Although her eyes were still trained on the dirt, the pronouncement came from her lips with absolute certainty. "You have freed me, my Lord."

The sandals shuffled closer to her, and a shadow moved over her body. Then a large hand met the crown of her head for a moment, before sliding down beneath her chin.

Yeshua gently lifted her head so that she was looking directly into the face of the One who had healed her. The One sent by Adonai whose feet she was not fit to wash.

"Daughter," He said, His eyes brimming with compassion as He curved both warm palms around her face, gazing at her eye to eye with the tenderness of a father looking on a beloved child. "Your faith has made you well. Go in shalom."

Another commotion arose as someone lifted a shout to let him through with a message for someone named Jairus. Confused and still trembling, Tikva watched as Yeshua stood in response to the servant's plea. Even as the messenger moved to address the Pharisee who'd come to Yeshua for his daughter's sake, Tikva mourned the absence of the Rabbi's warm palms on her face.

"I am sorry, my lord," said the messenger, his expression full of sympathy, regardless of the fact that he looked to be a servant to the man called Jairus. "There is no need to bother the

Rabbi any longer. Your daughter..." He paused, his eyes darting to Yeshua and then back again. "Your daughter has died."

Tears sprang to her eyes as she watched the respected man of God crumple forward into the arms of his servant. Tikva was immediately stricken with guilt. They were within sight of Capernaum here. Perhaps if she had not insisted on touching Yeshua He would not have stopped to look for her among the crowd or wasted His time speaking to her and instead made it to the girl's bedside. A girl had died because of Tikva's selfish desire to be healed this day.

But Yeshua went to Jairus, His arm once again going about the man's shoulders as he wept. At the same time, she felt the weight of someone's palm on her shoulder. She looked up to see that Simcha was standing above her, his twisted hand outstretched to help her to her feet.

"Come," he said, a gentle smile on his face and joyful tears in his own eyes that made it clear he'd heard every word between her and Yeshua. "I will take you home."

Just as she stood, her body replete with an abundance of energy she'd not felt for twelve years, she heard Yeshua speak to Jairus, a strange note of anticipation in His deep, rich voice. "Don't be afraid," He said to the grieving man. "Only believe, and she will be saved."

And with every part of her being, Tikva did.

CHAPTER TWENTY-TWO

✧

Beneath Tikva's feet, pebbles crunched and scattered as she spun in a circle with her palms upraised, faster and faster. It had not been since her wedding to Asa that she'd danced like this. The clapping and singing around her urged her on, making her joyous heart full to overflowing.

Sliding her arm into Na'ami's, her laughter refused to be contained as they twirled together in the center of the large circle of friends that had gathered around a crackling bonfire to celebrate. Not only had Zuri and Meira and the other traders joined the group of former beggars at their campsite on the beach, but the local potter and his wife and children had as well, bringing with them a number of friends and neighbors who were curious about the rumors they'd heard of Tikva's miraculous transformation.

Had it been only this morning that she'd awakened at dawn with a broken body? Even as Simcha had led her away from the crowd and from the One who'd healed her with only a touch, she'd felt the constant pulse of fresh energy moving through her limbs. No longer forced to shuffle along the road like an old woman, she'd had to restrain herself from slipping away from Simcha's side to run all the way back to the potter's house, calling out like the little boy had the day before, informing everyone within hearing distance of her miracle.

Not only had the blood ceased, which she had confirmed as soon as she'd been able, but there was no more persistent ache in her bones or in her mouth, and Na'ami and Chavah had exclaimed over and over that she was no longer dangerously pale but instead glowed with health and vitality. She longed for a mirror to see the changes to her countenance for herself, but regardless of the way she looked, inside she felt whole, full of life, as ebullient as a new bride.

Seated on the ground, with his twisted leg outstretched, Simcha clapped along with the rest, his deep voice joining in the psalm of praise to Adonai. Tikva wondered whether he was disappointed that he'd missed his own chance to meet with Yeshua, but the sparkle of pleasure in his brown eyes as he watched her dance certainly concealed any lingering regrets he might harbor. The image of him charging toward her accusers with his crutch outstretched like a valiant warrior would be one she cherished for the rest of her days. If not for his courage and sacrifice, she would still be just a collection of shards and splinters held together with a handful of fraying threads.

Once the song ended, she collapsed in a breathless but blissful heap on the beach next to Simcha, the pleasant ache of exertion in her muscles a stark contrast to the bone-weariness she'd carried around with her for so long.

Hiram launched into one of his new fisherman's tales, his wide palms waving about as he described how Levon had nearly been knocked overboard last night by a wayward sail. Laughter and good-natured jesting ensued as Levon responded with his own embarrassing story to entertain the gathering. Somehow becoming employed as a fisherman had loosened his once-silent lips, and he had the group in an uproar over his story of stealing Hiram's tunic while he'd been bathing in a stream.

Although Tikva had been happy to share her experience with Yeshua with all the newcomers to their celebration, she was glad the gathering's attention had shifted away from her for a few moments.

Simcha leaned close, his voice in her ear. "I could watch you dance all night."

A shiver of something new moved through her at his nearness. "I am tired," she replied, but at his slight frown she continued, "but a wonderful sort of tired. My poor feet are not used to this much excitement."

His gaze moved slowly over her face, as if taking each of her features one by one. "It is extraordinary," he murmured. "You look radiant. Almost like the beautiful girl I used to spy on long ago."

A flush of warmth met her cheeks. "I feel almost like that girl again. I cannot explain it…it's as if every part of me has been…reborn."

"I believe it," he said, then covertly brushed a hand over hers, making her startle. "Even your skin is warmer."

"I can never thank you enough for what you did today," she said, then frowned, her gaze dropping to his lame foot. "Especially when it meant that you missed your own opportunity with Yeshua."

He placed a finger beneath her chin, causing her to look up. "What was important to me is that *you* were given the chance to come before Him, Tikva. I told you before that I am content with my lot in life."

She nodded, accepting his statement but still wishing that this man who'd done so much for her would be granted another chance to experience the same wonder she had as her body was restored by Yeshua.

"However..." His hand dropped from her face, his brown eyes darting away. "The question is, are you content with it?"

"What do you mean?" she asked, unnerved by his obvious unease.

"You agreed to marry me yesterday, Tikva. But that was before..." His voice trickled off, but she knew he meant to say, *Before you were healed.* "I want you to know that if being bound to a lame man is too—"

"No," she interrupted. "Simcha, do not say another word. I am not marrying a lame man. I am marrying the most honorable man I've ever known. A man who threw himself in the path of my accusers to make it possible for me to reach Yeshua. There is nothing in my heart but pride that I will soon call you 'husband.'"

A broad grin spread over his face. "And I will be doubly blessed to call you wife and mother to my child, just as soon as we return to Ptolemais."

Thinking of Adina as her daughter made her heart swell with joy, but at the name of her hometown, a new thought occurred to her. "What happened to those men? The ones who know my father and were shouting at me?"

Frowning again, Simcha removed his hand, moving it to his own thigh, which he began to knead, as if it pained him. She wondered if he'd injured himself in his desperation to protect her this morning. "I think that they, like all of us, were stunned by what happened. As soon as Yeshua demanded to know who'd touched Him, they ceased their protests, likely thinking He meant to chastise you for your audacity."

"I feared He would as well," she said, remembering how she'd thought of her own father's disdain in that instant and how vastly different Yeshua's treatment had been. She could still feel the warmth of His hands on her face and the depth of compassion in His kind eyes.

"I only saw them once more," said Simcha. "Just as the rest of the crowd began moving on to follow Yeshua and the Pharisee. The three of them stood watching you walk past them, with their jaws hanging open. It was evident even then that something miraculous had occurred. They no doubt recognized the same transformation we see in you."

She wondered what the men might tell her father when they returned to Ptolemais. They'd come here to gather evidence against Yeshua, but would they return with stories of the miraculous instead? And how would her father react to the news that she had been healed?

All day thoughts of her family had welled up, along with nervous anticipation at the prospect of telling them what had happened here. Would her restoration cause them to embrace her once again, or had too much damage been done? She longed to feel her mother's arms around her again. Perhaps now that would no longer be an impossibility.

Drawn back into whatever loud and ridiculous tale Hiram was now spinning during her silent musings, Simcha did not seem to notice when Tikva slipped away from the group, heading down to the water's edge to dip her sore feet in the coolness. Ankle deep, she stood facing east, listening to the sound of the gentle waves against the shore and tracking a far-off fishing vessel as it glided toward the horizon. Turning her face downward, she watched the tiny ripples around her legs stretch in ever expanding circles, marveling that these quiet waters were the same ones that Yeshua had calmed with only the sound of His voice. She'd heard that voice with her own ears, and she prayed that she would never forget the tone of it, nor the expression on His face as He crouched down to look into her eyes and speak to her with such empathy, heedless of the hard-hearted accusers at her back. Whether He was the long-awaited Messiah or not, one thing she knew—any king who would bend down in the dirt to lift her up was the kind of king she would be happy to serve.

A flicker of movement to her right caught her eye and, turning her head, she caught sight of three figures walking on the shoreline toward her. A flash of recognition jolted through her at the familiar posture and sure stride of the One at the center of the group. It was Yeshua! She glanced back at the circle of friends and strangers back on the beach, wondering if they'd spotted Him as well, but some sort of jesting argument between Hiram and Chavah was keeping their attention away from the One with whom she'd had a brief but earth-shattering encounter only a few hours before.

She held her breath as He came closer, but He halted about twenty paces away to converse with His companions. Their animated voices echoed across the water, as did an unexpected laugh from Yeshua's lips, the sound seeming to wrap around her like a familiar embrace.

Thank You, whispered her heart. *Thank You for restoring me. Thank You for breaking my chains and bringing me back to life.*

Then, as if He'd heard the innermost thoughts in her soul, His head turned her way, and His eyes met hers, even as His companions continued to talk to one another. Her grateful heart pattered and flipped as she wondered whether Yeshua would close the distance between them, but instead a huge grin spread across His face, one that made her feel that He, too, rejoiced over the very healing He'd gifted her. She felt her own lips respond in kind.

Simcha! The reminder that he sat here on the beach, only forty paces from the Man who could heal his body too caused her to gasp and twist around to search him out in the crowd. But he was so engaged in a conversation with his new friend, the potter, she could not catch his eye.

Looking back at Yeshua, she gestured toward Simcha, praying that the Rabbi would understand that someone else was in need of His touch as well.

Yeshua's gaze moved toward her future husband, whose crutch was beside him on the pebbled beach and whose twisted hand lay atop his bent knee in full display.

How wonderful would it be for Simcha to stride into Ptolemais without that crutch! With his head held high and his restored fingers woven into hers, he would pass by all those who'd mocked him over the years, their mouths sealed shut with astonishment.

But, to Tikva's dismay, instead of closing the gap between Himself and the man she'd unknowingly come to love over the years, Yeshua looked back to her and gently shook His head. The image of Simcha's victorious return melted into disappointment at the slight gesture.

Tears sprang to her eyes as a silent *why?* formed on her lips. After healing her and erasing all the pain she'd endured, He would leave Simcha to suffer humiliation and hardship?

The corner of His mouth quirked as He met her gaze, and she recognized conflict in His expression. But then He repeated the shake of His head.

Not yet, came a whisper deep within her soul, one that spoke with the same divine authority that had calmed the waves.

Tears trailed down her cheeks as she acquiesced. She did not understand why it was not Simcha's time to be healed, but she would accept it nonetheless. Who was she to question the plan of Adonai?

After one more gentle smile that communicated an ocean of love and understanding, Yeshua slipped His arms over the shoulders of His friends and led them back in the opposite direction, another glorious laugh floating behind Him as He responded to whatever jest one of the men had spoken.

Tikva watched them fade into the distance and then returned to the circle of celebration to sit at Simcha's side, wondering whether she'd ever again see the face of the Man who'd changed everything.

CHAPTER TWENTY-THREE

◆

Chavah pressed a basket into Tikva's hands. "I wish that I had more to send you off with than just some dried fish and a few loaves of bread," she said.

"We are grateful," said Tikva, handing off the basket to Simcha, who tucked it into the trader's wagon next to the pots of dried fruit, beans, and the rolls of flax Zuri and Meira were bringing back to trade in Ptolemais. "Not only for the fish but for all your kindnesses while we were here."

Chavah kissed Tikva's cheeks with the same tenderness she did her own daughter. "Adonai brought you here," she said. "And I pray that He will guide you safely home."

Na'ami embraced Tikva, and the two held on to each other for several moments. "I will miss you, my friend. I wish you were staying," she said, tears in her bright green eyes.

Part of Tikva wished for the same. She'd enjoyed such peace here on the shore of the Kinneret, among this group of unlikely friends. But she was also eager to return to Helena and Adina in Ptolemais. She missed the tang of salt in the air and the clamor of foreign tongues in the marketplace—a marketplace that she would no longer be forced to avoid.

A spasm of nerves rushed through her at the thought of walking through her hometown. Would the people there still jeer and whisper? Would the children still throw pebbles at her back? Or would they see the flush of health on her cheeks, the strength in her gait, and the change in her demeanor and believe that she had indeed been healed?

She shook off the thought. It mattered not whether the people of Ptolemais believed. *She* knew the truth, and she would hide in the shadows no longer. Although it had taken a few days since her healing, she'd finally begun to feel more comfortable lifting her head as she walked down the streets with Meira. She vowed that when they returned, she would work proudly alongside Helena at the pottery stall and swallow any fear of meeting the eyes of their customers.

"Perhaps one day we will see each other again," she said to Na'ami, kissing her clear, smooth cheek.

"I pray it is so," said the young woman, stepping back to look between Tikva and Simcha. "But until then, I wish you great joy and shalom in your new life together."

Once goodbyes had been offered to Hiram and Levon, who both were yawning after a long night of fishing, and to the generous potter and his family who'd been so kind to let them encamp within their courtyard, Simcha and Tikva took up their places alongside the traders' wagons, and the group set off on the road that would lead them away from Capernaum.

She'd not seen Yeshua or His men again after her brief encounter on the beach, but the story of the little girl who'd been raised from the dead had saturated every corner of the town. From what they'd heard the next day, Yeshua had accompanied Jairus to his home and found the household already in mourning, the ululating cries of the women filling the air. But instead of being deterred, Yeshua told them the girl was merely sleeping and asked to be shown to her chamber. The strange statement had been met with laugher and derision.

A couple of weeks ago Tikva too would have scoffed at the idea that it would take only the sound of Yeshua's voice to cause the girl's lungs to pull in a breath, for her heart to begin to beat again, and her eyes to open. But if His voice could calm a storm and the barest brush of His tzitzit could undo twelve years of brokenness to her own body, then Tikva had no doubts that Jairus's daughter had indeed been rescued from the clutches of the grave.

After seeing the depth of the Pharisee's grief as he crumbled upon word of her death, she could only imagine the immeasurable joy on his face when his child sat up on her deathbed and asked for something to eat, as if only an hour before a physician had not declared her deceased.

On the road that day Tikva had been devastated that her touch had made Yeshua stop to seek her out, making Him too late to save the girl, but now she wondered if Adonai had meant it to be so, in order to display Yeshua's power to its fullest. If so, she was grateful to have played a part in such an awe-inspiring story.

One thing was for certain—since the recovery of the little girl and Jairus's public recounting of the miracle, there had been no more calls in the square for Yeshua to be expelled from the town. But people were fickle, as she well knew, and the tide of public opinion was easily swayed. Only time would tell whether Capernaum would continue to be a harbor for Yeshua and His followers or whether He would be forced to continue His work elsewhere.

Once their little caravan crested the final hill that would lead them out of the valley, Tikva took a few moments to pause and look back toward the Sea of Kinneret. The sun was still fairly low in the sky, but it glistened on the mirror of the waters, making the entire valley glow with golden morning light and making every shadow around her flee. Although the rustic Galileans were held in little regard within the bustling, modern cities of Caesarea, Ptolemais, and certainly Jerusalem, to her this beautiful region and its people were nothing less than a treasure. For it was here that her darkness had been swallowed up in light.

The words of the prophet Isaiah came to her, rising up like a song of benediction for their journey home.

"Nevertheless, there will be no more gloom for those who were in distress...he will honor Galilee of the nations, by the Way of the Sea, beyond the Jordan—The people walking in darkness have seen a great light; on those living in the land of deep darkness a light has dawned."

Recalling that the rest of that passage spoke of a Child who would grow to one day sit on the throne of David, who would establish and uphold justice and righteousness in their land, the rest of her doubts about who Yeshua might be fled along with those shadows. Rushing to catch up and take her place next to Simcha, she turned her face toward home, still wondering how an army of the blind, the lame, and the beggars would change the world but fully assured that somehow, they would.

CHAPTER TWENTY-FOUR

"Abba! Tikva!"

Regardless that the past few days of walking had sapped a large portion of her newly restored energy, at the sound of her name being called by her favorite girl, Tikva's limbs buzzed with anticipation. Adina hurried toward her with arms outstretched. Without thinking, Tikva began to run, something she had not done in twelve long years.

Simcha's daughter plowed into her and wrapped her arms about Tikva's waist. "You are back!" she cried. "I missed you so much!"

Tikva gripped Adina's body close, pressing kisses to her temple. "I am," she said. "I missed you as well."

Adina tilted her head back, looking into Tikva's face. Slowly, wonder crept into her expression, and her grin grew impossibly wider. "You ran!" she said. "You ran to me!"

Throat aching with emotion, Tikva nodded. "That I did."

"And your face is so full of color." Adina reached up to stroke Tikva's cheek. "And warm."

Tikva pressed her own hand over Adina's. "I am no longer sick," she said. "Yeshua took it all away."

"Truly?" asked the girl, with a squeak in her voice. "You are well?"

"I am."

Over Adina's shoulder, Tikva caught sight of Helena making her way toward their little reunion, along with a few curious neighbors who'd emerged from their homes at the sound of Adina's cries.

"Go to your abba," said Tikva. "He has missed you so much."

Adina obeyed, running back to meet Simcha, who dropped his crutch to lift his precious daughter off her feet and crush her to his chest for a moment. A pang of regret nicked Tikva's heart at the reminder that if he'd been healed he would have been the one to run to his daughter instead of her, but she clung to Yeshua's silent assurance that although Simcha might endure his limits for a time, someday it would not be so.

Helena approached slowly, her eyes taking in Tikva as if she'd never seen her before. Meira had offered Tikva a small, beautifully polished hand mirror, procured from another trader out of Egypt, to see the changes in her countenance for herself, so she knew what her mother-in-law was seeing now.

Her skin was no longer ashen and pale but glowing and tanned from her days walking alongside Simcha. Her eyes no longer held a sunken, hollow look to them but instead glinted with the sparkle of life. Even her hair no longer hung limp and dull. Her curls had returned to their once untamable mass around her face and shone with sun-burnished tones.

"Can it be?" asked Helena, her hand outstretched to place a palm on Tikva's cheek. "Did He...?" Her words dissipated into awe.

"Yes," said Tikva, answering the question Helena seemed unable to finish.

A choked sob came from her mother-in-law's lips.

"I have so much to tell you of our journey," said Tikva, noting that a small crowd had begun to gather about them in the street. These were the faces of people who had for the most part shunned her over the past twelve years, neighbors who'd brushed past her without a word of shalom, children who'd slung names and stones at her. But instead of cowering from their curious gazes, she placed the smile of the Man who'd changed her life in the center of her vision and lifted her chin to speak. "But for now I will say this—the Man named Yeshua, whom many here have heard rumors about in recent months, has restored my body to full health."

Gasps of surprise went up all around them, giving her courage she'd never thought she might have.

"I am no longer zavah," she said, ignoring the flush of warmth on her cheeks, because she knew that everyone in this town had been aware of her condition, thanks to Tamar's vicious gossiping. "I have indeed been healed."

Although her heart pounded at the feeling of so many eyes on her after hiding for so many years, her transformation was nothing that could be ignored. She knew that she would be the subject of much curiosity over the next few days and weeks, and she vowed to give testimony to what she had experienced. Unlike He had with Na'ami, Yeshua had not asked her to stay silent, so she would spend the rest of her days telling anyone who asked about the Man who'd stopped on His way to raise a little girl from the dead to offer her the gift of life as well.

Simcha appeared at her side, with Adina tucked beneath his arm. "Come," he said, with a smile that she finally allowed herself to feel all the way down to the soles of her feet. "It is time to go home. I have something I'd like to discuss with my future mother-in-law."

As Helena's mouth dropped open in surprise, Adina let out a whoop of joy that echoed down the street and directly into Tikva's heart.

◆

Tikva hesitated at the top stair, heedless of the line of murmuring women behind her. Gazing down at the clear water, she took a moment to remember the last time she'd stepped into this mikveh, just after her wedding to Asa. Back then she'd taken for granted the act of washing her body within this consecrated pool, not pausing to consider what a blessing it was to be a daughter of Abraham, nor the privilege it was to take part in the ancient festivals set aside by Adonai as one consecrated to Him. But standing here, after enduring the humiliation of having to prove the change in her body by presenting seven days of clean rags, she knew that she would never again brush aside such weighty matters.

From the moment she'd touched Yeshua's tzitzit she'd known she was healed, and had felt the cleansing of her soul as she'd spoken her belief, but once she immersed herself in this pool of living water, fed by the aqueduct that carried water from the mountain springs far to the north, she would finally be considered clean in the eyes of the world. No more would she be banned from the synagogue, and no more would she fear brushing up against others in the marketplace or suffering the accusing eyes of those who'd blamed her. And tomorrow, freshly consecrated for the ceremony of marriage, she would become Simcha's wife, without reservation. And all because of a Carpenter from Nazareth.

With the image of Yeshua's smile in her mind, she placed her bare foot down onto the first step, bracing against the chill of the mikveh. Descending each stair with care, she plunged her body deeper and deeper into the icy water until it reached the top of her waist. Curling her arms around her abdomen, she whispered another word of thanks to Adonai for what had been accomplished within the depths of her body, and even thanked Him for those few precious months when another heartbeat had fluttered beneath her own. She took comfort in knowing that Adonai had gathered that tiny, unfinished life into His arms, and prayed that in the world to come, she might be privileged to do the same.

Then, with a psalm of gratitude flowing in her heart, she took the final three steps and immersed herself in the pool. When she arose, dripping and shivering, she was finally clean.

CHAPTER TWENTY-FIVE

⟡

Tikva ran her fingers through her still-damp hair. A shiver whispered up her spine as a brisk gust of wind swept by. Even the warmth of the sunlight on her back had yet to fully thaw the chill of the mikveh from her bones. Taking in the elaborately carved cedar door in front of her, one she'd carelessly rushed in and out of hundreds of times, she pulled in a breath and knocked.

Perhaps it had been a mistake to come here directly after her washing. Or perhaps it was a mistake to come here at all. But when she heard the swish of sandals against stone inside the house, she knew it was too late to change her mind. The door swept open, and just across the narrow threshold was her mother, eyes wide and mouth agape.

"Tikva." Her name huffed from her mother's lips like a sigh, a prayer, and a sob wrapped up in one word.

Tikva trembled, no longer because of the sea breeze on her damp skin and clothing but because she could barely contain the instinct to fall into her mother's arms.

But there was no need for such restraint, because her mother's grip on her own had snapped. She dropped the linen cloth she'd been holding and dragged Tikva into a tight embrace, her body shaking as she kissed her daughter's crown, forehead, and cheeks.

"Oh, my precious girl," she said. "I am so glad you are here." But as she did so, she looked up with a start, her gaze moving up and down the street to search for witnesses to their reunion.

All the effervescent joy Tikva had enjoyed in the past few moments dissolved into hurt. Her mother may be glad to see her, but she did not want anyone else to know that her outcast daughter had come to her door.

"Come inside," she said, drawing Tikva across the threshold and closing the door tightly behind her. "It is best if we speak privately."

Sorrow and wounded pride welled up, overflowing her lips. "I am *clean*, Imma. Unless I've been defiled by some unknown thing or unconscious sin between the mikveh and here, there is no longer any need to shun me."

Her mother's eyes dropped closed at the censure in Tikva's voice. "It has been a long time, Daughter. There are still many questions in people's minds. Much talk in town and at the synagogue."

"People will always talk. Always raise a brow at the unknown. But if the truth is that I have been restored to health and am no longer zavah, then why do you pull me inside as if I am still something to be ashamed of?"

"I was never ashamed of you," her mother said, her tone surprisingly strident. "You are my daughter. I have loved you since the moment I first felt you move within my belly. Nothing you have done or will do would change that."

"Then why?" Tikva cried out. "Why would you cut me from your life? I needed you." Her voice rose as she spoke, her hands shaking. "You knew I was suffering, bleeding, broken, and yet you refused to see me again!"

"Hush!" Her mother darted a palm out to cover her lips. "Your father is just down the hallway, resting. He's been ill these past few days."

Tikva yanked her mother's hand away. "Why, Imma?"

"Because I am a coward," she responded, her words a hiss. "A coward and a spineless woman full of fear." She swept a gaze around the finely appointed room. "If it wasn't your father telling me that he could not risk his reputation with the synagogue, then it was Tamar and the other women reminding me of how much I stood to lose." She covered her face with both hands, shaking her head. "No. I have no excuse."

Pain, anger, and compassion all warred within Tikva as she waited while her mother gathered her composure. There was no doubt that she was remorseful over what she'd done to Tikva, but why had she never revealed as much over the years. A note? A messenger? Something?

"Come, sit with me for a few moments," said her mother as she wiped tears from her cheeks. For the first time Tikva noticed that her mother's face seemed inordinately drawn, shadows painted beneath her eyes, and here in the house her customary head scarf was abandoned, so Tikva was able to see that there was more gray than brown in her mother's hair now.

Up close, a few age spots dotted her hands, and a bevy of fine wrinkles surrounded her eyes and lips, as if from many years of frowning. It seemed as though twelve years of regret were actually written across her skin.

Her mother led her to a low couch, bedecked with a large assortment of soft pillows fashioned from finely woven cloth, lined up with precision along the wall. With a quick glance about the room Tikva noted that it was little different from when she'd been a girl. Not a thing was out of place, and the limestone floor had been scrubbed to gleaming with the special cleaner her mother made from a mixture of natron and various floral oils. Tikva had spent many an hour on her hands and knees in this very room, swirling the fragrant mixture across the tiles with a rag, polishing it to a sheen that would please her fastidious mother. She wondered if her mother had been tending this expanse alone since Tikva had been married. One glance at her mother's dried and cracked palms answered the question. This fine house that she'd given up so much for, including her own daughter, was nothing more than a burden, one that seemed to be sucking the life from Tikva's once-vibrant imma.

"Tell me what happened," said her mother. "How did this…" She brushed her palm over Tikva's face, a look of awe coming over her. "What did that Rabbi do to you?"

"So you know then? About Yeshua and who He is?"

Her mother sighed. "I do. Three of your father's friends came knocking on our door a few days ago, before you returned to the city. They told him that you'd been healed, but truly,

I did not believe it until I saw your face just now. The changes are incredible."

The changes inside Tikva were even more startling, but she didn't know how to explain the earthquake that had rocked her soul. So instead she told the story of the journey she and Simcha had taken to Capernaum, of how they'd nearly missed Yeshua a number of times, and how she'd come to be on her face in the road before the Healer.

"If I did not see you with my own eyes I would not believe the tale you've just told me," said her mother. "And this Man, this Yeshua, what did He ask in payment for healing your body?"

"Nothing," said Tikva. "I would have had nothing to give Him if He did. I'd used the last of my dowry money, which Helena had secreted away for me, to go to a Greek physician a few months ago, one who did more harm than good." She brushed a finger over the scar on her arm from Damianos's blade, one that would forever remind her that waiting on Adonai was always a better course than relying on people.

Her mother closed her eyes, lips pursed as if attempting to control an outburst of emotion. "I knew you were destitute. I begged your father, pleaded with him to send you money, food, anything. But he refused, saying that your husband's family was responsible for your welfare." Rare anger flared in her mother's eyes. "And once you began working with the lame potter—"

Tikva snatched her hand from her mother's grip. "His name is Simcha. He is the most honorable man I have ever met, and it was his generosity that kept Helena and me alive over these many years. And after tomorrow I will have the honor of calling him my husband."

Her mother's lips were parted in shock as she surveyed Tikva's determined expression.

"I meant no offense, my sweet girl. I have been told that indeed Simcha is a kind man. What I meant to say was that once you began working with Simcha, I wanted so badly to come to the market and purchase items, but your father forbade me to even do that. However"—she lowered her voice—"I paid a few people over the years to do so for me. And a few of my friends, who knew how stiff your father's spine was when it came to you, purchased goods from there as well. He is very talented, your Simcha." Her mother smiled and gestured to a tall vase that sat atop an ebony table in the corner, one with a shimmering green glaze that Tikva had watched her betrothed apply many, many times over the years.

Tears stung her eyes.

"I could have done more," said her mother, frustration building in her voice. "I should have done more. As I have said, I have no excuse other than my fear and pride. It is my fault that you have suffered for so long. Perhaps it was even my pride or vanity that caused such a curse in the first place."

Tikva thought of the Pharisee's daughter and how she had suffered death, only to be raised to life by Yeshua's voice.

"No, Imma," said Tikva. "It was not your fault that I suffered from that affliction. I too blamed myself, wondering what offense I'd committed against the Almighty. But there was no accusation from Yeshua when He healed me. He did not demand that I repent of whatever had caused the bleeding. He simply had compassion on me, healed me, and made me new, without condition.

"And in fact," she continued, "I've come to realize that I do not wish away the struggles that I have endured. For as difficult as it was to push through my exhaustion to work for Simcha, I have learned to truly love it, and now that I have more strength, I can be of even more help. I have formed a deep friendship with Helena, who has been my rock all this time, which I would not otherwise have had. I have been given the pleasure of helping raise Simcha's daughter—the sweetest, brightest girl I've ever known—and even though I thwarted his offer of marriage years ago, Simcha has protected me and provided for me, without expecting anything in return. I have learned so much over the years. I have been tested and tried, and now I have seen miracles with my own eyes. I have seen a woman afflicted with leprosy made whole, and I have felt the healing touch of the man whom I believe to be the Messiah. So no, I do not regret the suffering I have endured, for without it, none of that would have been a part of my story. And somehow, after being touched by Yeshua, being truly seen by Yeshua, I no longer hold any bitterness in my heart toward you, or Abba." She smiled, knowing deep within her bones that it was the truth. "I forgive you."

Her mother began to weep, and Tikva wrapped her arms about her, her own tears coursing down her face. She'd not realized how deep her wounds had gone when it came to her mother and father, and she suspected that she'd pressed the hurt and anger down so far that it was only the Healer's touch that could have reached it. By the time the two of them had dried their faces and Tikva took her leave of her parents' home, the last of that bitterness had been cleansed from her heart.

Making her way back toward the tiny room she and Helena would no longer share after tonight, for the both of them would move into Simcha's home after the wedding, she felt even lighter and more free than she had in the hours after she'd been healed. She decided to change her course and head into the market to purchase wedding gifts for both the man who would become her husband and the girl who would become her daughter tomorrow. Her mother had forced a small pouch of silver shekels into her hands before she left, insisting that although it could not make up for the past, she wanted to do something to bless Tikva and Simcha on their wedding day.

But just as she was dreaming of purchasing a set of new carving tools for Simcha and a swath of fabric to make a new tunic to accommodate Adina's swiftly lengthening legs, a man and a woman stepped into her path. Filthy from head to foot, the young couple stood in front of Tikva, desperation plain on their faces.

"Please," said the man, his palm uplifted, "do you have a coin to spare? Our children are hungry."

The woman refused to meet her eye, shame written on every line of her skeletal face. Tiny red dots along her neckline, around her ears, and across her forehead made it clear that her body was infested with fleas.

Stomach turning over in sympathy, Tikva's gaze was drawn to the two children huddled in the shade of a building behind them, watching expectantly as their parents begged for their bread. Dressed in rags, both the boys' eyes were hollow and sunken and one of them had only stumps where his arms should be.

Just as she had all those years ago when she'd gone to this market with a full purse around her neck, Tikva could feel the weight of the coins against her skin. She smiled, knowing exactly why Adonai had led her to her mother's door this day. She had plenty within her pouch to provide this family with clothing and food, and more.

"I do indeed," she said, reaching out to slip her arm through that of the woman. The woman flinched, shocked, no doubt, that anyone would deign to touch her grimy, flea-ridden body. "But before I give it to you, I'd like you to come home with me. Let's share a meal, and I will tell you of someone you need to seek out. His name is Yeshua."

CHAPTER TWENTY-SIX

Tikva looked around the tiny room, her gaze traveling over the dirt floor where her pallet and Helena's used to lie, to the small square of sunlight where she used to stretch out her soiled rags each morning beneath the window, and the crumbling ceiling where at one time a treasure was hidden. Although she'd despised this room and the losses it reminded her of, she could not help but feel a little sad to leave it for good.

"He will be here soon," said Helena, as she tightened the papyrus cord on her rolled-up pallet. "Are you ready?"

"I am," said Tikva. "However, I still have trouble believing that this portion of my life is over."

Helena gave her an understanding smile. "You deserve only good things from here on, daughter."

Tikva was not so naive as to believe that she would be forever untouched by hurt, fear, or pain, but she hoped that this day would be the start of many filled with joy.

"I would not be here if it were not for you," said Tikva. "I can never adequately make clear how much your love has meant to me over these years. I was blessed the day I married Asa, because you came into my life."

Helena's brows pulled together, her mouth drawn into a deep frown. "I have failed you many times. The midwives, the physicians, the Greek—"

"Hush," said Tikva, going to her mother-in-law and wrapping her arms about her. "That is in the past, swept away by Yeshua's touch. We both were flailing about, looking for solutions. I do not fault you for doing everything you knew of to try and save me. You stood by my side when everyone else fled. And you have been both mother and father to me over these past years."

A knock sounded at the door, and Tikva's heart leaped at the sound.

"Your bridegroom has arrived!" Helena brushed tears from her face and kissed Tikva's cheek before winking mischievously. "I shall turn my back while you greet him."

Flushed with embarrassment at the sly look on her mother-in-law's face, Tikva giggled as she moved to open the door for Simcha, heart light and eager to take in the sight of the man who would be her husband this day.

But it was not Simcha who stood at the door with a nervous expression on his face and his hands twitching at his sides, but her father.

"Abba," Tikva gasped. Unable to form words in her shock, she stared at him. Lifting a hand to stroke his beard, something she remembered him doing whenever he was out of sorts, his eyes darted to the right and the left. He wore his distinctive dark robes, but not, she noticed, the ostentatious turban he'd worn every day in public since she was a little girl.

"May I come in?" he asked, then cleared his throat. "I...I have something I must say."

Had her mother sent him here? Surely he had not come to halt her wedding to Simcha? Her heart raced at the thought before she reminded herself that since the moment she'd been given to Asa he had no authority over her. His opinion on her marriage to a lame man had no bearing, this day or any other.

"I must go speak with Reuvah next door, Tikva," said Helena behind her, with a comforting squeeze on her shoulder. "I'd like to say goodbye before we depart."

Nodding, Tikva let Helena slip past her and did not miss the stern look her mother-in-law directed toward her father. Tikva managed to squelch a smile at the protectiveness Asa's mother maintained. The woman had been a force of nature as a rich woman, but poverty had done nothing to erode her backbone. Tikva had no doubt Helena would have no fear in taking him to task if necessary, Pharisee or not.

Tikva stepped back to allow her father entry, keeping her chin high as he crossed the threshold and entered the hovel she'd been living in, the hovel she'd not have been forced to endure but for his pride and neglect.

He said nothing as he took in the meager belongings now stacked against the wall awaiting their move to Simcha's home.

He heaved a sigh and crossed his arms over his chest. "I have been told that you were healed," he said.

"I am," she responded. "I washed in the mikveh yesterday, so I can no longer defile you."

His jaw worked back and forth, and he nodded. "When Nathaniel and his friends returned from Capernaum, bringing news that this Galilean Rabbi had healed you, I did not believe them."

"Well, now you can see for yourself," she said, gesturing to her face. "You saw me before, when I was little more than bones and skin. Everyone tells me I look like a different person."

His gaze moved over her face, and Tikva restrained the urge to fidget during the slow perusal. *Let him look*, she thought. *Let him see what Yeshua has done.*

"It is astounding," he said. "Your mother told me it was like the day you married, as if you were glowing from the inside."

She smiled at that, knowing that was exactly how she felt, and glad to know that her mother perceived it too.

"I have heard from Nathaniel and the others what happened that day, but I'd like to hear it from you as well. If you'd be willing to tell me."

Astounded by the obvious curiosity in his tone, she blinked at him. "If they already told you, then why ask me?"

He pulled at his beard again. "They say crowds follow this Man wherever He goes, desperate to hear Him speak, and that the people lift Him up as the Messiah."

"That is true."

"And what do you think?"

"I am a woman. One that you have shunned for twelve years. What does my opinion matter?"

He let out a long, slow breath. "I have been...reassessing a number of things, Tikva. And after hearing the things you told your mother yesterday—"

"You were listening?" she interrupted.

"I was. I heard your voice right after you arrived, so I listened by the door."

She lifted her brows. "I cannot count all the times I was chastised in childhood for doing the same thing."

Her father's lips twitched, as if holding back a laugh, before his expression melted back into sobriety. For as much as her father had wounded her, even that slight indication that he still valued her and found amusement in her spirit gave her the courage to speak.

So, after taking a moment to unwind her memories, all the way back to the day she stood before Simcha's pottery stall and heard the news of Asa's death, she began to tell her story, her courage expanding with every word.

She told him of the suffering she'd endured, of the pain of being shamed and cast out by the people of Ptolemais. She told him of the many supposed healers and their useless promises. She told him how Helena had spent most of what she had left after the sale of her beautiful home to help her. Although it made her wince at the thought of revealing how she'd put her hopes in the Greek healer for a time, she told him of Damianos and the horror she experienced in his household. Then, once she'd laid out all the ugliness of the last twelve years, she told him of Yeshua. Of the conflict between the Pharisees in Capernaum. Of the crowds and the purported healings and of the first time she'd caught sight of the Galilean Rabbi. By the time she began her description of the day she'd been healed and the words from the prophets that had come to mind during that time, her father had gone ashen.

"I did not know that you'd retained so much of the Tanakh," he said, astonishment evident in his voice.

"Don't you remember that you used to allow me to listen in when you taught my brothers? I recited those words inside my head and heart whenever they recited them aloud. Those lessons, even though they were not meant for me, have never gone away."

"And by these things you are convinced that this Yeshua is the King who will sit on the throne of David?" he asked, incredulous.

"I am no scholar, Abba. I am no learned rabbi like you. But I know what I saw. I looked into this Man's eyes and saw His compassion and sincerity. I saw Na'ami's leprous face before she was healed and witnessed the transformation afterwards. And I felt the power move through my body at His slightest touch. I believe that He was sent by Adonai. I don't know how it will happen, but I believe that someday, He will indeed govern from Jerusalem."

He was silent for a long while, his eyes on the dirt floor. When he finally met her gaze, he nodded. "I have much to ponder. I sent Nathaniel and the others to bring back evidence against the Man, and they returned even more confused than before. And I must admit that I, too, am conflicted."

"How can you be conflicted, Abba?" She lifted her palms in supplication. "Look at me. I am no longer ruined. My body no longer bleeds constantly. My strength is that of the young maiden I was all those years ago. How can you even doubt?"

"I don't doubt that you are changed, Tikva. But a Carpenter as the King of the Jews? That is taking things too far."

Sighing, she dropped her arms. Her father was nothing if not stubborn. "Time will tell. One way or the other, I do not think it will take long before we know for sure."

"Yes, I suppose that is true. Although the debate that is raging in the synagogues with regards to this Man seems to only have just begun." He was silent for a few more moments, stroking his beard. "Your mother tells me you are marrying the potter today."

She lifted her chin, half-daring him to speak a word of censure. "Yes. Simcha is an honorable man, and I will be proud to stand by his side for the rest of my days."

"Yes… Nathaniel told me of the way he came to your defense in Capernaum. But can he provide for you? I've been told his business has suffered some setbacks. Now that things have changed for you, perhaps you should return home?"

Her mouth gaped, struck as she was by his suggestion and all it implied—restoration to her place among her family, acceptance by the people of Ptolemais, and an end to the day-to-day struggle for her daily bread. But close on the heels of her astonishment, defensiveness roared to life.

"It does not matter how few shekels we have," she said. "I will trust Adonai to provide for our needs. You may have sold me to Asa's father to fund your precious synagogue, but this time I am choosing to bind myself to a man because there is no other I could ever want as my husband."

She thought of the beggars she and Helena had fed last night, here in their tiny home, and the words of gratitude they offered when she turned the entire amount her mother had given her earlier into their palms before sending them on their way to Capernaum to search out Yeshua for themselves.

"Rich or poor, it matters nothing to me," she said with a smile. "As long as I have Simcha and Adina, then I will be content."

Just as a mixture of shame, awe, and profound confusion came over her father's countenance, a second knock sounded. Without hesitation, Tikva opened the door, all thoughts of her father's suggestion melting away at the sight of Simcha and Adina standing hand in hand on the other side of the threshold.

"We've come to bring you home!" said Adina, bouncing up and down on her toes. "And a few of our neighbors have been preparing a feast!"

Simcha's smile was nearly as large as his daughter's. "I will send one of the men to retrieve your belongings later this afternoon." His eyes twinkled with mischief. "But you will be coming with me now, wife."

The word sang in her heart as she returned his smile. "I am more than ready."

Behind her, her father shifted his feet, the sound of his sandals scraping against the packed dirt floor causing Simcha's gaze to flit over her shoulder in surprise.

"I must take my leave," her father said. "Your mother will be wondering where I've disappeared to since I've been ill for the past few days."

Tikva crossed the threshold, making room for her father to pass by and moving to stand by Simcha's side to show her unequivocal determination to remain there. Adina slipped around to weave her fingers into Tikva's, and her heart squeezed, replete with love for the girl.

Much to Tikva's surprise, instead of striding away, angry at her refusal to capitulate to his request, her father turned to face her and her bridegroom.

Then, as if twelve years of willful separation had not come between them, he reached out a hand and placed it atop Tikva's head. Tears immediately began streaming down her face as her father opened his mouth to speak a blessing over her, her marriage, her new daughter, and the home they would all share. Trembling, she peered up as his words trailed off, amazed that his eyes, too, glimmered with emotion.

"Thank you, Abba," she whispered, too overcome to say more.

He nodded, his lips pressed together, and then he turned away, nothing of the haughty Pharisee in his posture as he walked down the street with his head bowed. Yeshua had changed everything for Tikva in one small touch, but she suspected that the healing He'd set into motion had only just begun.

EPILOGUE

One year later

"There's another one, coming from the south!" called Adina, shading her eyes from the glittering reflection of the sun off the blue waters below. "Look how many sails it has."

Tikva snagged her arm, pulling her away from the lip of the bluff. "Careful, daughter, or you'll tumble over the edge and find yourself in the sea."

Since Tikva and Simcha married last year, she and Adina had made a habit of coming to her favorite spot every so often to watch the ships come into port and guess from which far-flung land they'd originated.

"I think it might be from Alexandria," said Adina, "by the shape of the bow."

"You are likely correct," replied Tikva. "If we did not need to prepare for our journey today, we could go down to the harbor and confirm it once it arrives."

"We leave in the morning?" asked Adina, all suppositions about the many boats that streamed in and out of Ptolemais's busy port pushed aside by thoughts of their upcoming journey.

"Yes, Zuri and Meira will be leaving at dawn, so we must be prepared tonight." Tikva was thrilled about the prospect of traveling with her trader friends again. And even more exciting was that this time their destination would be Jerusalem itself, where the people of Adonai would gather in a few days to celebrate *Pesach* in remembrance of their forefathers' escape from Egypt.

She'd not been able to attend the ingathering celebration for nearly fourteen years and was eager to step foot back inside the sacred city high in the hills of Judea. She was determined to wash in the Pool of Siloam, make her way up the long road to the holiest of places, and finally, after all this time, set foot within the boundaries of the Temple courts. And, thanks be to Adonai, there was no longer any hindrance to her doing so.

"I wish Helena were coming with us," said Adina, her jutting lower lip reminiscent of her younger years.

"I do too," said Tikva, brushing her windblown hair out of her eyes. "But she must continue selling in the market while we are gone. Now that your father has taken on two more apprentices, we must sell enough pottery to sustain more than just our own family. Perhaps next year."

Tikva's healing at Yeshua's hands had done much for Simcha's business. In contrast to the days when Helena had to practically beg customers to peruse the offerings on her table, now there was a steady flow of those curious to hear the tale of Tikva's transformation, the by-product of which were more sales of Simcha's work. And although it had taken Tikva many weeks to be comfortable looking others in the eye and not shying away from the attention, she never tired of speaking of what Yeshua had done for her.

Adina sighed, turning back to the water. "I cannot wait to see Jerusalem, but I wish we could take a ship there instead of riding in a donkey cart."

Tikva laughed. "If only that were possible, sweet girl."

"Will we see Yeshua?" she asked.

Tikva's heart thumped an uneven beat of anticipation. "Nothing would make me happier. It's been said He is frequently seen there, but it is not certain that we will cross paths with Him." However, Tikva prayed it would be so, because she longed to see the face, and hear the voice, of her Rescuer once again.

Many were the rumors of the Rabbi over the past year, each seeming more impossible than the last and some completely contradictory, but it was clear that His time in Galilee seemed to be over, and His work was now centered in Judea. Although more and more whispers of Messiah were spoken alongside His name, Tikva had still not heard anything about Yeshua building an army—just more healings, more miracles, and more angry Jewish leaders. But in her bones she felt that the day was coming soon when all would be revealed. Perhaps even this year, while they were in Jerusalem!

A warm and familiar strong arm wound about her waist, pulling her from her musings. "I've come to fetch my girls," said Simcha, and then he pressed a kiss to Tikva's cheek.

"Abba!" said Adina, coming over to lean against her father's shoulder. "I've counted thirteen boats this morning. One we think might even have arrived from Alexandria."

He chuckled, shaking his head and grinning at Tikva. "I fear our daughter is far too enamored with the sea. We must keep an eye out whenever my brothers come to visit, or one day she'll stow away on one of their vessels."

Adina grinned up at her abba, mischief glittering in her eyes. It seemed that every day Tikva noticed changes in Adina that proved she was transforming into a beautiful young woman before her eyes, one who not too far in the future would become a wife herself.

"Is everything in order for our departure?" asked Tikva, to push aside the wistfulness such thoughts provoked.

"Yes," said her husband. "Helena has it well in hand. My younger apprentices are terrified of her, so I am sure they'll keep up with production until I return."

"Of that I have little doubt," said Tikva. "She likely enjoys having more people to order about than just the three of us. You should have seen the way the servants in her house scurried about as if their sandals were on fire whenever she entered a room."

Simcha tipped his head back to laugh at the image, and Tikva and Adina joined in. They all adored the woman they'd invited into their home and family but knew her quirks all too well.

Once their laughter melted away, Adina trotted off to pick a few of the yellow and pink flowers that had burst into being in the past few days, saying she wanted to leave the woman she regarded as a grandmother with something to brighten their empty house while they were gone.

"Does this vista still inspire melancholy in you?" asked Simcha, as the salty breeze wound about them and ruffled the long grasses atop the bluff.

Tikva was unsurprised that he'd noticed such a thing, for her husband seemed to always be keenly aware of any shift in her spirit, and she'd revealed everything about her past to this steadfast and generous man she adored.

"Perhaps a bit," she said on a sigh. "I never fail to remember Asa, along with our lost child, when I come here."

He brushed his palm up and down her arm, a reassurance that her words did not wound.

"But it also reminds me that those sorrows have now been eclipsed by so many joys. I will always mourn them," she said, then smiled up at her husband. "But Yeshua washed all my bitterness away, along with my affliction."

After pressing a kiss to her lips, Simcha pulled her closer to his side, his hand slipping from the curve of her waist to stroke his three long fingers over her gently rounded belly, where a new joy grew beneath her heart.

* * *

AUTHOR'S NOTE

A number of years ago, before I was a published author, I entered a writing contest. My story told of a woman whose entire life was altered by the brush of fingers to a few threads, a tiny moment that changed everything.

You see, in my own personal Bible study, I'd become fascinated by all the brief encounters with Jesus during His time on earth, and my writerly mind spun with questions of what happened *after* such life-changing brushes with the divine.

I was also inspired by a sermon I'd heard about how the corners of the garment, with the knotted fringes (tzitzit) attached, were called the "wings" or *kanaph*, and how any Torah-observant synagogue attendee would have been familiar with the passage in Malachi that prophesied the Sun of Righteousness appearing with "healing in his wings." So when the time came to select the subject of my contest entry, I knew I had to explore the connection between this beautiful Messianic prophecy and the woman who touched the hem of Jesus's garment.

I wrote a thousand-word short story about that moment as the Savior is on His way to a seemingly much more urgent matter. An unnamed woman presses through the crowd, knowing that if they knew who she was and why she was there, they might stone her for making them unclean. But she is so desperate for healing that she refuses to give in to those fears.

When the idea for the Ordinary Women of the Bible was proposed to me, I was overjoyed at the chance to dig further into this woman's extraordinary life, to imagine what it would have been like to live as an outcast—even among the outcasts—for so many years. To be excluded from participating in the religious traditions that were so much a part of the identity of the Jewish people during that era. To know that your life was slowly ebbing away and no amount of money or prayer or effort could change that.

Until Jesus.

I am so grateful to my writing partners, Nicole Deese and Tammy L. Gray, for lending me their imaginations as I plotted the details of Tikva's life, and for cheering me and bolstering my spirits during the wild time I was writing two books at once. Also for Tina Chen, Ashley Espinoza, and Joanie Shultz, who beta-read this book and graciously offered their honest thoughts and critiques.

And to Susan Downs and the wonderful team at Guideposts Fiction, thank you for giving me the opportunity to spin my short little glimpse of this fascinating character into a fuller story! The more I put flesh on Tikva, the more in awe of her courage and faith I became, and the more I appreciated the goodness and mercy of the Rabbi who stopped, looked her in the eye, and called her daughter.

FACTS BEHIND
the Fiction

✦

THE HEM OF HIS GARMENT

Scripture tells us in Matthew 9:20–21 that a woman (who, in this story, we've called Tikva, which means "hope" in Hebrew) came up from behind Jesus and "touched the fringe of his robe, for she thought, 'If I can just touch his robe, I will be healed'" (NLT).

The Greek word used for "fringe" (of His cloak) is *kraspedou*, which is translated "tassel," "fringe," "hem," or "border" in English translations of the Bible. Biblical scholars suggest that this is the same kind of fringe known as *tzitzit*, still worn today on the corners of Jewish men's garments and prayer shawls (*tallit*, singlular; *tallitot* or *tallits*, plural). As a rabbi and a Jewish man in the first century, Jesus likely followed the teachings of the Torah, such as this one from Numbers 15:38–39 (NIV): "Throughout the generations to come you are to make tassels on the corners of your garments, with a blue cord on each tassel. You will have these tassels to look at and so you will remember all the commands of the LORD, that you may obey them." So He might have worn this type of fringe on His garments, which is what Tikva would have reached out to touch.

TYPICAL JEWISH TASSEL (TZITZIT)

Similar language is also used in other places in the Gospels in relation to Jesus's healing of people:

- "She touched the fringe of his robe. Immediately, the bleeding stopped." —Luke 8:44 (NIV)

- "They begged him to let the sick touch at least the fringe of his robe, and all who touched him were healed."—Matthew 14:36; Mark 6:56 (NLT)

In Matthew 23:5, Jesus criticized the Pharisees for enlarging the length of their tassels (*kraspeda*) "for people to see" (NIV) in order to impress them.

ROMAN "CURES" FOR A WOMAN'S AILMENT

> "A woman in the crowd had suffered for twelve years with constant bleeding. She had suffered a great deal from many doctors, and over the years she had spent everything she had to pay them, but she had gotten no better" (Mark 5:25–26 NLT).

First-century Roman writer Pliny the Elder (AD 23–79) made it clear why Tikva—or any woman of modest means suffering from excessive bleeding—could run out of money long before doctors ran out of treatment options.

Pliny was still a boy, roughly ten years old, when Jesus healed such a woman. Decades later, Pliny wrote a thirty-seven-volume encyclopedia called *Natural History*. He devoted five of those books to health care, and he cataloged several dozen treatments for excessive bleeding like Tikva's.

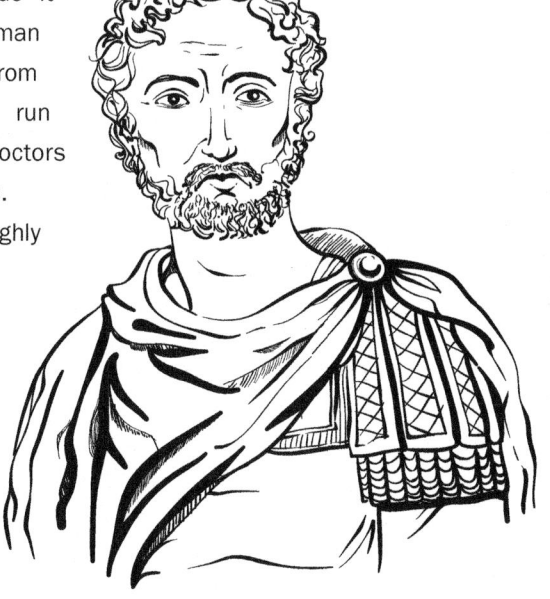

PLINY THE ELDER, NATURAL SCIENCE WRITER, HISTORIAN, AND MILITARY COMMANDER; BASED ON CESARE CANTÙ'S *GRANDE ILLUSTRAZIONE DEL LOMBARDO-VENETO* (1857–61)

HERE ARE JUST A FEW OF THE TREATMENTS PLINY SAID PHYSICIANS RECOMMENDED:

- Drink beaver oil mixed with honey.
- Crush several snails. Mix them with starch and the sap of the locoweed or the goat's thorn plant. Apply topically as a liniment.

MULBERRY

- Mix honey and vinegar with oil crushed from the mint-scented pennyroyal plant. Drink.
- Mix vinegar and water with juice extracted from a rose. Drink.
- Pluck a single mulberry fruit off a branch that is just beginning to bear fruit. Do this during a full moon. Don't let the fruit touch the ground. Tie it onto the woman's upper arm.
- Catch a spider in the palm of the hand as it's climbing up. Apply topically (presumably crushed dead). Note: Be careful. If the spider was descending, it produces more bleeding.

There were many more supposed cures outlined by Pliny. It is easy to see why Tikva's bank account would have been emptied in her search for a cure and why her desperation drove her to seek out Jesus, the Great Physician.

OBSESSING OVER RULES

Pharisees were among the most legalistic sects in Judaism. Pharisees represented one of several branches of the Jewish faith. Others included Sadducees and the monk-like Essenes, who apparently preferred to live in Essene-only communities.

Pharisees were staunchly legalistic and loaded with hundreds of extra religious rules that, despite not being in the Bible, they badgered everyone to obey. A version of these rules later became known as the Oral Law, an extension of the Written Law that appears in the Bible.

These extra rules were a bit like those we might find in a church manual today. Religious leaders crafted the laws to help people of faith know how to apply biblical teachings to their lives, but in the case of the Pharisees, it went too far.

FAREWELL, PHARISEES

Romans destroyed the Jerusalem Temple in AD 70, crushing a Jewish revolt. Suddenly, Jews no longer had a place to offer sacrifices and find forgiveness. Many Jewish rules revolved around worship at the Temple. Those rules, which Pharisees policed, instantly became obsolete. In time, so did the Pharisees. Rabbis emerged as new leaders. Local synagogues became the place for Jews to worship God and to offer sacrifices of prayer with "a broken and repentant heart" (Psalm 51:17 NLT).

PHARISEE PRAYING IN THE TEMPLE

UNCLEAN

There's a reason the bleeding woman who wanted Jesus to heal her "came up behind him through the crowd" (Mark 5:27 NLT). She was sneaking in. She wasn't supposed to be there.

She was not only ritually unclean—which means unfit to worship in the Temple—she contaminated everyone and everything she touched. They too became unclean and had to go through cleansing rituals. It was written into Jewish law (see Leviticus 15:25). Anyone who touched her became unclean. To become clean again: "You must wash your clothes and bathe yourself in water, and you will remain unclean until evening" (Leviticus 15:27 NLT).

No wonder Jesus shocked the unclean woman when He called her out, right in front of everyone. "She came shaking with fear and knelt down in front of Jesus" (Mark 5:33 CEV).

This woman "suffered for twelve years with constant bleeding" (Mark 5:25 NLT). That's how long she had been isolated—cut off from the touch of people and even from worshipping God in the Temple.

She trembled partly, perhaps, because she was afraid of what was going to happen to her for contaminating the Messiah.

As it turned out, she couldn't spiritually contaminate the source of spiritual cleansing. Jesus healed her before He said a word. Then He wished her well and sent her on her way, free of pain and her infirmity.

TOUCHING THE HEM OF HIS GARMENT

A SNAKE ON A POLE: THE SYMBOL OF HEALTH CARE

A familiar symbol of health care is a snake wrapped around a pole. There are only theories and ancient legends to shed light on how this symbol came to represent medicine and health care.

Many scholars believe that the snake symbol comes from Greek mythology. The oldest symbol shows just one snake on a stick. Physicians today know this symbol as the Rod of Asclepius (as-KLEE-pee-us), also called an *asklepian*. (Two snakes wrapped around a pole, topped with wings, was originally the symbol of the Greek god Hermes, though the image is also popularly used today as an emblem for medicine and health care.)

Asclepius, son of the god Apollo and a human mother, was a demigod linked to health care.

One theory suggests that the staff represented doctors walking to make house calls. As for the snake, it represented new life. That's because it could shed its skin and start over. Physicians also taught that snakes and toxic venom could have healing power.

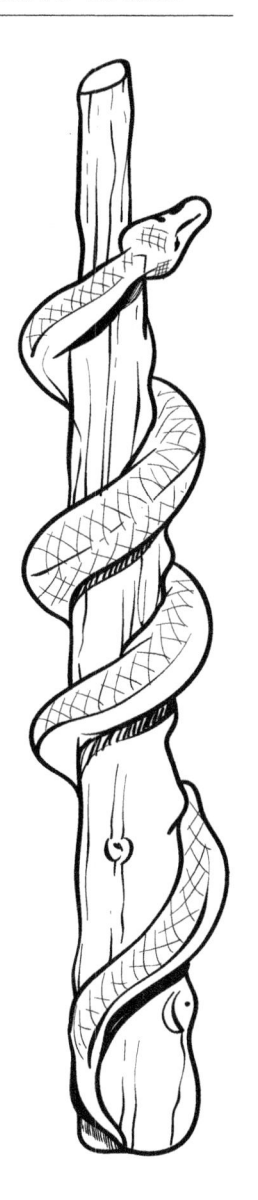

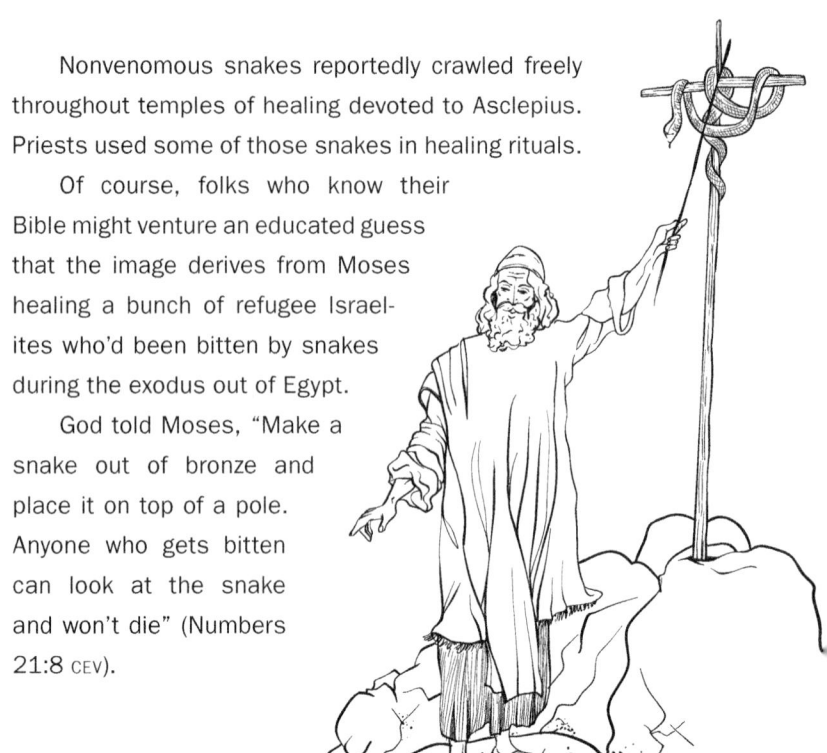

Nonvenomous snakes reportedly crawled freely throughout temples of healing devoted to Asclepius. Priests used some of those snakes in healing rituals.

Of course, folks who know their Bible might venture an educated guess that the image derives from Moses healing a bunch of refugee Israelites who'd been bitten by snakes during the exodus out of Egypt.

God told Moses, "Make a snake out of bronze and place it on top of a pole. Anyone who gets bitten can look at the snake and won't die" (Numbers 21:8 CEV).

MOSES HEALING THE ISRAELITES WHO HAD BEEN BITTEN BY SNAKES IN THE WILDERNESS

VILLAGE POTTER, THE PRACTICAL ARTISAN

In the rural villages of Galilee, where Jesus spent most of His ministry, no artisans were more important than potters, like Simcha in our story.

They supplied homes with clay ovens and oil lamps, along with jars that held water, wine, and expensive perfume for burial rituals. Potters also made huge jars to store household grain, other dry goods, and even valuables such as jewelry and contracts written onto pottery shards and scrolls. Some of the famous Dead Sea Scrolls, with ancient copies of Bible books, survived two thousand years in clay jars stashed inside caves.

A DIRTY JOB

Potters often built their workshops outside the village. The work was messy, and village folks didn't take kindly to kiln smoke twenty-four hours a day.

Making pottery wasn't just a matter of grabbing a fistful of clay and slapping it onto a potter's wheel. Potters had to prepare the clay first, sun-drying it and then beating out the lumps with a hammer and removing pebbles, twigs, and anything else that didn't look like pure clay.

With the clay cleaned, potters would add water and knead out air bubbles by stomping it with their feet. Then they'd fold the clay and mix it with their hands. Once more they'd let it sun-dry to remove excess water from the stomping and mixing.

A TYPICAL POTTER'S WHEEL FROM BIBLE TIMES

POTTER'S WHEEL

Potters often worked their clay on a potter's wheel. Much like a modern potter's wheel, it was usually built with two wheels connected by an axle. The potter turned the bottom wheel with his foot, and that turned the axle along with the wheel connected on top. On that top wheel the potter shaped clumps of clay into products for homes and businesses.

After firing, the clay object was then ready for whoever ordered it, or for selling or trading at the village market.

Apparently, potters didn't tend to get rich. One writer long before Jesus used pottery to illustrate poverty: "See how the precious children of Jerusalem, worth their weight in fine gold, are now treated like pots of clay made by a common potter" (Lamentations 4:2 NLT).

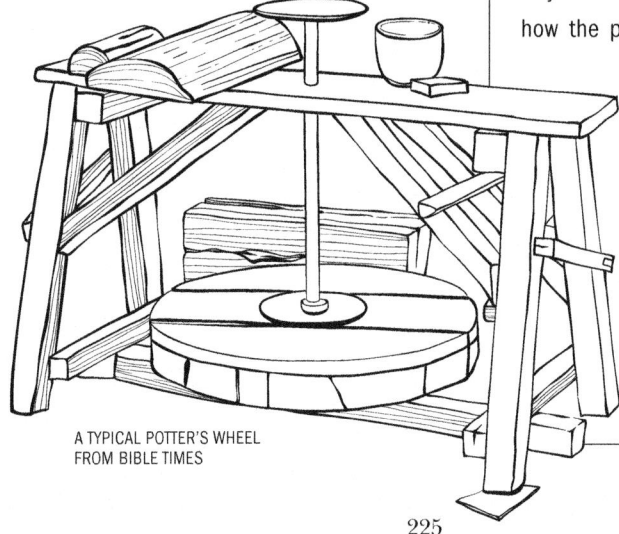

Fiction Author
CONNILYN COSSETTE

Connilyn Cossette is a Christy Award–nominated and CBA-bestselling author of biblical fiction. There's not much she enjoys more than digging into the rich, ancient world of the Bible, discovering new gems of grace that point to Jesus, and weaving them into an immersive fiction experience. She lives in North Carolina with her husband of over twenty years and a son and a daughter who fill her days with joy, inspiration, and laughter.

Nonfiction Author
STEPHEN M. MILLER

Stephen M. Miller is an award-winning, bestselling Christian author of easy-reading books about the Bible and Christianity.

His books have sold over 1.9 million copies and include *The Complete Guide to the Bible*, *Who's Who and Where's Where in the Bible*, and *How to Get Into the Bible*.

Miller lives in the suburbs of Kansas City with his wife, Linda, a registered nurse. They have two married children who live nearby.

Read on for a sneak peek of another exciting story in the Ordinary Women of the Bible series!

◆

THE ARK BUILDER'S WIFE: ZARAH'S STORY

by Tracy Higley

A chill breeze tunneled through the courtyard of the small temple, a hint of the coming darkness. The sun had dipped below the roofline of the moon god's temple nearly an hour ago. In the courtyard, those who spread their goods for sale on rough blankets and the half walls surrounding the sandy square were packing up what was left after a day of bartering.

And yet still Zarah waited, leaning against the wall as she had done for hours. Her fingers played over the smooth stones of her latest piece, ruby-red clusters set in delicate metalworking of silver, a piece as valuable as any she'd ever made.

She waited for Barsal, who had promised her four shekels for her finest work. Barsal, who flaunted his many cattle and his many children with equal pride and could well afford to pay for a necklace such as this.

Across the courtyard, a woman and her husband tied the last of their remaining leather goods into pouches strapped to a snorting donkey. The husband's hand rested lightly at the small of his wife's back as she closed the final pouch, and Zarah's heart twisted a tiny bit at the tender gesture.

Where was Barsal? Zarah scanned the street beyond the courtyard but saw only shoppers and merchants hurrying along ahead of the night.

The light was fading fast now, and it was already beyond the time of safety for traveling home, especially if she still carried the necklace. A woman alone in the dark in the city of Kish was likely to never see home again.

Not only Kish. Zarah pushed away the memories of the larger city Tikov, as evil a place as this city, even if the evil was cloaked in a veil of beauty.

The couple had finished packing up and walked their donkey across the courtyard. The woman nodded to Zarah as they passed. It was courtesy only. Zarah had never had many friends in this city, and now, years later, she had even fewer.

Barsal's wife, for whom she had made the ruby necklace, had once been a friend, but she had not seen her in years.

The couple slowed. "Not going home yet? It is getting late." The man's brows drew together in judgment.

She shook her head. "Waiting for a promised customer. I'm certain he won't be long."

The man shrugged and they moved on, arm in arm. The wife leaned her head against his shoulder briefly.

Zarah sighed and looked away. She remembered what it felt like to be a true partner to her husband. To work alongside each other, eyes on the same goal, one in spirit. She had known that sort of marriage once. But these past years had brought many changes.

The wind shifted again, bringing with it the sharp tang of the tannery, the odor warning her again that nothing good moved at this time of day. She wrapped her tunic more tightly across her chest, the necklace gripped in tight fingers inside its folds.

Enough. She could wait no longer. The city of Kish had given itself up to lawlessness years ago, and regardless of her husband's efforts to maintain some semblance of holiness before his God, the rest of the city had embraced a culture of violence, greed, and license.

She tugged at the multicolored scrap of fabric on the waist-high wall beside her and rolled it into a ball. The fabric had held her lesser pieces, already sold, earlier in the day. The coins were safely tucked into a leather belt beneath her tunic, but they were a pittance compared to what Barsal had promised.

Promised, but not delivered.

The courtyard was entirely deserted now. She was alone with night falling. She cursed her own stupidity in staying so long. Only the deep desire to bring home such a welcome sum of money had kept her. Such a sum could buy enough lumber for weeks of building. Her contribution would be recognized and appreciated. It might not be the affection they had once shared, but gratitude was at least something.

She hurried into the street, then kept to the courtyard wall as she turned toward home. It was a long walk to the edges of Kish where she lived, between the city and the farmland beyond. Not much of their farmland was left any longer, of course. Not since *The Project* had begun.

The mud-brick houses of the street presented blank faces as she passed, but here and there through an occasional open doorway she caught a glimpse of lamps being lit and families circling their tables.

With her head down against the wind and her thoughts on home, the *smack* into a dark cloak knocked her backward and stole her breath.

"Barsal!"

He loomed over her, smelling unwashed and grinning like a man who had been drinking too much.

Zarah lifted her chin. "You are late. I waited. Waited too long."

Barsal folded bulky arms across his chest. His eyebrows lifted in derision. "I keep my own schedule, woman."

A tickle of self-protection made her push forward, skirt Barsal, and walk on. She did not like his mood.

Barsal grabbed her arm from behind and twisted her to face him. "Where do you think you are going?"

She yanked her arm from his meaty clutch. "Home to my husband. You may call there tomorrow if you are still interested."

"Ha!" Barsal's laugh was more menacing than amused. "No, I believe I will take the goods now." He pulled at that hand still hidden under her tunic. The necklace tumbled from her fingers to the dirt.

Zarah bent to retrieve it.

Barsal snatched it before she had a chance.

"Fine," she said. "You have your necklace. Please pay me, and we can go our separate ways before it gets any later. Neither of us wants to be out at night, I am certain."

Barsal held the necklace up to the dying light and examined it. "Well done, little priestess. Well done."

"Do not call me that."

Barsal chuckled. "No? Is that not what you are? Moon god priestess?"

"You know very well that I am not." She swallowed hard against the anger. Against the memories. How had Barsal learned of her past?

"Hmm." Barsal tucked the necklace into a pouch at his waist. "Perhaps no longer. Now you belong to another holy man, I suppose. But once…"

His leering smile turned her stomach. "Pay me, Barsal, and let us finish this."

"Oh, we are finished, little priestess. We are finished."

A stab of anxiety threatened her composure, and she fought to keep her head high and her voice calm. "I don't think you would want word getting out that Barsal did not pay what he owed."

Barsal laughed, his dark eyes piercing her. "And who would believe the word of a worthless woman that even the moon god Sin did not care to keep?"

Zarah took a step backward. "What do you know of it?"

He shrugged one shoulder and patted the pouch that held the necklace. "I make it my business to know things. Tikov is not so far away. I trade there often. And I ask questions."

Zarah ran a fumbling hand through her hair, then clenched her hands together to still their trembling. The temple built to honor the moon god.

Sin, or Nanna as he was sometimes called, held nothing but evil memories. "There is nothing to know. It was long ago."

"Hmm. Not so long that your husband wouldn't be curious to hear of your life there."

"I had no life there."

Barsal eyed her up and down, as though taking in her words and understanding their true meaning.

Yes, Tikov was long ago. And yes, it was not a life. More like a walking, waking death.

"Still," he hissed, "I should think the stories I heard would be good for telling around the fire, to your husband and your three sons."

She saw the scene played out before her in a flash. The four men, hearing the truth, mouths agape, eyes turning to her in condemnation.

Zarah threw her shoulders back and tried to return his menacing look, despite her inner trembling. "Enough of this, Barsal. You've had your fun. Pay me what you owe, then leave me alone."

Barsal laughed. "You don't seem to understand. My payment is my silence. That is all the payment you will receive, and more than you deserve for such a small bauble."

"I made that piece with extra care, out of my years of friendship with Etana. It is worth four shekels and you know it!"

"Ah, yes, but what is my silence worth?"

Two figures slid from a dark slot of an alley between houses. Barsal eyed them and then pushed past Zarah. "It is a time for being indoors. You would do well to hurry home."

She grabbed at his cloak and hung on. "You cannot do this, Barsal. I beg you! That money is needed."

He backed up and raised an arm over her head as though to strike her.

She loosened her grip on his cloak.

The two men who had come from the alley approached behind Barsal. They were both young, with a hungry look about them and their eyes on her.

She'd had no fear that Barsal would harm her. Only cheat her.

But these two, they looked as though they would take whatever money she did have left from the day's bargaining and leave her for dead in the street.

Zarah watched the two figures over the shoulder of Barsal, her hand involuntarily sliding into the folds of her tunic, fingers curling around the pouch of coins.

Barsal seemed to sense that her distress had moved from his actions to something even more sinister. He whirled to face their would-be attackers, hands fisted at his sides.

"Go home!"

Did Barsal think that the loudness of his voice would be enough to scare them?

The taller of the two jutted his chin toward Zarah. "Your wife should be off the street by now."

"She is not my wife."

Zarah's stomach clenched. The only thing more dangerous than a woman on the street at night was one who was there alone, without a protector. Women did not simply get assaulted in this city—they disappeared altogether.

The other of the men who had not spoken circled to stand behind Zarah. He was short but broad, with a stubbled chin and stringy hair.

A cold sweat chilled her skin, and she fought to keep from crumpling.

"Then you should be at home as well."

With a glance and a shrug at Zarah, Barsal pushed past the taller man and disappeared into the gloom, leaving her to the mercy of the two.

In the beat of silence that followed, she swallowed against the fear and tried to find her voice.

"Thank you." She nodded to the man still facing her. "I had begun to think he would not leave me alone. I am in your debt." She moved to walk past him.

He stepped into her path. "The streets are unsafe."

She tried to smile. "Then I will hurry home."

"Not alone."

Zarah frowned. There was nothing threatening about the words, nor the tone.

From behind her, the stubbly one spoke. "You are his wife, are you not?"

"As he said, I am not—"

"No, not Barsal. You are the shipbuilder's wife."

Zarah sucked in a breath. That was what they called him. The "shipbuilder." There were only a few who did not regard her husband's project with derision. Many even believed that it invoked the wrath of the local gods. "We have done nothing to—"

"Your husband deals justly." The taller man before her stepped aside and swept a hand toward the street ahead. "The least we can do is bring his wife home to him safely."

Zarah exhaled, but it was not time to be unguarded. The city was full of liars. She could not be certain these two truly had any regard for her family.

But she walked forward, and they followed at a respectful distance that did not feel threatening. Surely if they wished her harm they would not simply follow, would they?

She quickened her steps, past the line of mud-brick homes in the center of the city, toward the outskirts. Beyond the end of the main street, across their field, she could see the glow of her rooftop kitchen's cooking fire. One of the girls must have started the evening meal's preparation without her.

She risked a glance back to her escorts at the edge of the field.

They both drew to a stop at her look.

"I am nearly home now." She nodded. "Thank you."

She watched their eyes move upward, beyond the house and its glowing cook fire, to the hulking outline that lay beyond, barely visible now in the sinking light. The massive shape that defined everything in her life, that consumed the attention of her husband as surely as the cook fire consumed the dung chips that kept it burning.

There was nothing more to be said. She turned and hurried across the field, knowing that they would not follow.

She should have felt gratitude for the safety they had afforded her, but in truth she felt empty and heartsick, for she knew what was to come—returning home without the money that Barsal should have paid her.

Outside the house, the wooly sheep Muti greeted her with a soft *baaa*.

She stopped to wrap her arms around his thick middle and feel the scratchy softness of his wool against her cheek. "Good evening, old friend." No matter what reception she received from the family inside this house, Muti always welcomed her.

With a final pat to Muti's head, she pushed forward with resolve and opened the door.

"There you are!"

A flurry of skirts and dark hair met her just inside the door and pulled her inward. The soft glow of lamplight outlined Salbeth's petite figure, and the girl's arms went around her, clutching Zarah to herself.

The embrace was unexpected on so harsh a night, and tears welled before Zarah knew what had happened. She returned the girl's embrace. Salbeth had the smell of freshly baked bread in her hair, and Zarah breathed in the homey warmth of it.

The girl pulled back and examined Zarah's face. "I saw you from the rooftop, coming across the field. Saw those men following you." She gripped Zarah's arms. "Are you well? Did they have ill intent?"

Zarah tried to smile. "I am fine. They—they knew of our family. Seemed to have respect and wanted to see me safe."

Salbeth's expression of concern turned to frustration. "What were you doing out so late?"

Zarah shook her head. "It's nothing. Come. Is dinner prepared? The men must be hungry."

She led the way inward, wishing she could spend some time in the cool peacefulness of the leafy central garden, but instead she climbed the narrow stairs to the second floor, which was open to the dark sky just beginning to show its stars.

They were all there. Her family.

The muscular Shem, who leaped up to embrace his wife, Salbeth.

Witty and entertaining Japheth, with his loyal wife, Aris.

Ham, always eager to get something done, and the lovely but petulant Na'el.

And Noah. Zarah's husband.

None of them had met her at the door but Salbeth. The three wives of her sons were well able to cook the meal and keep the house and do all the things that once were her responsibility. Did any care enough to worry, to wonder where she had been?

Behind her, Salbeth whispered in her ear. "The men have just come in from the work. None of them know you were not at home."

Ah. And yet the knowledge that she was not missed did not feel comforting.

She took her place on the mat beside Noah, accepted the loaf of bread he passed to her, and tore a large hunk from it. The loaf had risen too high and was hollow inside. Perhaps Salbeth still had much to learn about the ways of the kitchen. She glanced at the girl, but Salbeth had already settled into the crook of Shem's arm and seemed unconcerned with the hollowness of her bread.

As Zarah would be, if she had a husband who was attentive for reasons that had nothing to do with bread.

"Well?" Noah's eyes were on her as she passed the loaf to Na'el. "Will we have funds enough for the next phase?"

So, it was already time. Time to speak of her failure. To make it clear in front of her entire family.

She ripped a piece of bread with her teeth and chewed it slowly. She felt as hollow as the bread tonight.

"He… He refused to pay me."

Noah set down the crock of wine he had been sipping. "What?"

"Barsal. He—he took the necklace. But he refused to pay me."

Noah was already getting to his feet.

Japheth pulled him back to his mat. "Father, there is nothing that can be done tonight."

Noah growled. "That man is a scoundrel. He makes money in every dishonest way he can think of, and then he thinks to cheat me?"

Zarah looked away. Barsal had cheated *her*, not Noah. But of course, it was all the same.

"We were to use those funds for the rest of the needed wood. We have only the rooftop and some interior pens to build before the ark is finished. And we are running out of time."

His words lingered in the air, his sons saying nothing.

It was well established that only Noah seemed to hear from his God. Shem, Ham, and Japheth were willing to work, willing to build, because their father housed them, fed them, clothed them. It was a family project, yes, but not because the sons believed the words of their father. Only because they relied upon his provision for them and their wives.

And Zarah? Did she believe? Believe what Noah had been saying for all the years that he had been building?

It had been easy at first, when they still had at least some friends, and grain in the fields. These past few years, though, when everything had dwindled to nothing, she had struggled to hold on to faith.

"We will go to him tomorrow," Noah was saying. "We four men." He nodded around the circle to his sons. "He will pay us what he owes."

Zarah said nothing. Would Barsal pay? He was a dangerous man to confront.

And would he speak to Noah of the truths he knew? Of her past that would make her even less significant in the eyes of her family?

A NOTE FROM THE EDITORS

We hope you enjoyed *The Healer's Touch: Tikvas's Story*, published by Guideposts. For over 75 years, Guideposts, a nonprofit organization, has been driven by a vision of a world filled with hope. We aspire to be the voice of a trusted friend, a friend who makes you feel more hopeful and connected.

By making a purchase from Guideposts, you join our community in touching millions of lives, inspiring them to believe that all things are possible through faith, hope, and prayer. Your continued support allows us to provide uplifting resources to those in need. Whether through our communities, websites, apps, or publications, we inspire our audiences, bring them together, and comfort, uplift, entertain, and guide them. Visit us at guideposts.org to learn more.

We would love to hear from you. Write us at Guideposts, P.O. Box 5815, Harlan, Iowa 51593 or call us at (800) 932-2145. Did you love *The Healer's Touch: Tikvas's Story*? Leave a review for this product on guideposts.org/shop. Your feedback helps others in our community find relevant products.

Find inspiration, find faith, find Guideposts.

Shop our best sellers and favorites at
guideposts.org/shop
Or scan the QR code to go directly to our Shop

Find more inspiring stories in these best-loved Guideposts fiction series!

Mysteries of Lancaster County
Follow the Classen sisters as they unravel clues and uncover hidden secrets in Mysteries of Lancaster County. As you get to know these women and their friends, you'll see how God brings each of them together for a fresh start in life.

Secrets of Wayfarers Inn
Retired schoolteachers find themselves owners of an old warehouse-turned-inn that is filled with hidden passages, buried secrets, and stunning surprises that will set them on a course to puzzling mysteries from the Underground Railroad.

Tearoom Mysteries Series
Mix one stately Victorian home, a charming lakeside town in Maine, and two adventurous cousins with a passion for tea and hospitality. Add a large scoop of intriguing mystery, and sprinkle generously with faith, family, and friends, and you have the recipe for *Tearoom Mysteries*.

Ordinary Women of the Bible
Richly imagined stories—based on facts from the Bible—have all the plot twists and suspense of a great mystery, while bringing you fascinating insights on what it was like to be a woman living in the ancient world.

To learn more about these books, visit Guideposts.org/Shop

Printed in Great Britain
by Amazon